DESTINY

Josephine Brennon was untapped depths of emotion. Crazy and unexpected as it was Hannibal wanted to . . . lay down with her, in the room right above them. He had no business thinking what he was thinking, but being rational was the last thing on his mind. He wanted to make love to a woman he had no idea existed until this day. Something about the woman who sat across from him felt one hundred percent right.

"You shouldn't have hired me, Josephine."

His voice was heavy with sorrow. Even if she would have him in her bed, he was a drifter. Drifters never stayed in one place for long.

Her smile never changed. It was her eyes he could not read. She made her question sound like an absurdity. "Are you a criminal?"

"No."

"Did you run away from your responsibilities?"

"If you mean a wife and kids, no."

With mystery in her eyes, she measured the power in his hands. Slowly, Josephine smiled until her whole face lit up. Hannibal's heart stuttered. The brightness of her smile transformed her face. Her smile drew him to her with the promise of a thousand secret pleasures. She leaned across the supper table to touch one knuckle of his hand with the tip of an index finger.

"I believe I chose well."

BOOK YOUR PLACE ON OUR WEBSITE AND MAKE THE ARABESQUE ROMANCE CONNECTION!

We've created a customized website just for our very special Arabesque readers, where you can get the inside scoop on everything that's going on with Arabesque romance novels.

When you come online, you'll have the exciting opportunity to:

- View covers of upcoming books

- Learn about our future publishing schedule (listed by publication month and author)

- Find out when your favorite authors will be visiting a city near you

- Search for and order backlist books

- Check out author bios and background information

- Send e-mail to your favorite authors

- Join us in weekly chats with authors, readers and other guests

- Get writing guidelines

- AND MUCH MORE!

Visit our website at
http://www.arabesquebooks.com

DESTINY

SHELBY LEWIS

ARABESQUE
BET BOOKS

BET PUBLICATIONS, LLC
WWW.MSBET.COM
WWW.ARABESQUEBOOKS.COM

ARABESQUE BOOKS are published by

BET Publications, LLC
c/o BET BOOKS
One BET Plaza
1900 W Place NE
Washington, D.C. 20018-1211

First Printing: April, 2000
10 9 8 7 6 5 4 3 2 1

Printed in the United States of America

For Steven and Randal

Acknowledgments:

To Antoinette Reed for allowing me to share our private joke about the name Ivy Didwiddee. Antoinette and I have been friends since we were twelve. In all these years, I never knew her real name was Ivy. I discovered her true name while we were having one of our Girls-Only weekends together. As we were laughing, we happened to be on a street named Didwiddee. The two names stuck and I promised Antoinette I'd use them one day. Sister-friend, I kept my word.

To Maria Elena Hayes for her encouragement and support while writing this story. She edited *Destiny* in its totally raw stages and offered detailed advice that was both unexpected and extremely welcome. When I asked her to read the early manuscript, I had no idea she was a business/English major. Talk about fate! Thank you, Elena.

To Judy Schatz for the character name Shirley Louise. Judy and I are coworkers. She often shares ideas with me regarding plot themes and character names. One day, she hit on the name Shirley Louise and the name worked well for this story. Thanks Judy, aka Steel Magnolia.

To Almeda Bess. I enjoy your honesty and your

company. Thanks for making me laugh and for being my friend.

To my sister, Toni. She surprised me with a visit the weekend *Destiny* was due to the publisher. She stayed up with me all night, literally proofing as I pulled the final draft off the printer for mailing. She had no idea I needed her, and yet something told her to come. She's a year younger than I am, but sometimes the connection between us is strong enough for us to be twins. Thanks, Sis.

To my sons, Steven and Randal. I've been writing for ten years and they've been unsung heroes the whole time. When the boys were small, they kept busy and played around me while I struggled to be published. After I was published, they attended book signings and promoted my work because they felt it was the right thing to do. These days, I also work as a medical secretary which means when I get home, the last thing I want to do is write a book. This is where the boys really kick in. Not only do they keep the house in order, but when it's cold, I come home to a fire. When I'm tired, they make coffee we often drink together. I could not ask for greater sons than Steven and Randal. Like Sethe says in *Beloved*, "(They are) my best thing."

To my husband, Steve. At last, we've come full circle.

"Coincidence, if traced far enough back, becomes inevitable."

—*Inscription on a Hindu temple near New Delhi and quoted by Carl Gustav Jung*

ONE

Early December

It was Sunday afternoon in Half Dead, a small town still standing only because it was the exact center of the southwestern state of Texas. It was a town where liquor stores had more believers than either the Baptist or the Methodist church.

Twenty-eight-year-old Hannibal Ray was having the time of his life in a fight against the town loudmouth, Mac Bishop. The opponents were well matched, both men six feet tall and physically fit from years spent hauling brick, laying cement, felling trees, and doing other muscle jobs.

The fun-loving crowd around the big men cheered their approval of the fight. The rowdy sound of the cheering crowd excited Hannibal, who had nothing else to do that afternoon but brawl in the dirt with Mac, a man so focused on winning he made it a point to lock eyes with Hannibal every chance he got during their fight.

Mac's drive to win thrilled Hannibal, who gave his all during any battle he fought. He figured there was nothing better than an honest fight to get his blood flowing. Right now the blood flowed from his mouth, down his chin, onto the skin of his swollen-eyed opponent.

With a smirk on his arrogant, sweating face, Hannibal taunted his adversary. "Had enough?"

Mac never bothered to answer. He knew this tactic of Hannibal's well. He knew it well because in the past, he had lost several fights because of it. If he allowed Hannibal to break his focus with taunts, he would become too angry to fight with the skill he needed to win. The only problem was, no matter how hard he concentrated on winning, Mac never did.

Instead of doing what he usually did by responding to the taunt designed to distract him, Mac took aim at Hannibal's well-traveled boots and spit on them. The long stream of spit was colored brown from chewing tobacco.

Mac almost laughed at the disbelief on Hannibal's dirty face. His outrage took Mac all the way back to one late summer afternoon when the men were fourteen years old, neither one of them worried about what tomorrow might bring.

The two childhood neighbors had gone fish-

ing at Old Man Miller's pond. At the end of
a day spent snagging catfish and bluegill at
Hannibal's side, Mac had pulled out a pack of
chewing tobacco from the front pocket of his
cut-off jeans.

Hannibal was so upset with Mac, he
snatched the whole pack of tobacco from his
friend's dirty fist and tossed the pack into the
pond. It was a fresh pack. The fight between
the boys that late August afternoon only
stopped when Old Man Miller shot his rifle in
the air twice in order to scare the boys apart.

Mac later learned why Hannibal hated chew.
Hannibal hated chew ever since his daddy lost
half his face to cancer after spending years of
storing tobacco in his left cheek. Because of
the way his daddy lost part of his face and later
his life to cancer, Hannibal hated all tobacco
use. As men, the tobacco spit changed the at-
mosphere of the fight.

Hannibal stopped being cocky, his way of
playing up to the crowd in the circle around
them. It was time to get serious with Mac, time
to end their Sunday afternoon brawl. Besides,
after ten minutes of thumping on each other,
both men were tired.

Mac's stale breath scented the air between
the two fighters. A once-promising basketball
player, he had wasted his chance to play with
the pros because he failed to finish his senior
year of high school.

It took little time for him to find out that

ex-promising athletes from small towns like Half Dead were plenty. To his dismay, his much-celebrated ball-handling skills were not great enough to get him into college. He was not disciplined enough to work his way into the pros.

This is why he fought with Hannibal for the umpteenth time since grade school, starting with their fight at age seven when Hannibal had called Mac an idiot and meant it.

Mac fought Hannibal as a boy because Hannibal made him actually feel like an idiot. He fought Hannibal as a man for the same reason. It seemed to Mac that he would never score one point higher than his former best friend. It was as if the two adversaries had been born to fight each other, as if it was their destiny to fight.

Mac figured Hannibal had everything, yet he was the kind of guy who wanted nothing. Easygoing, plain-living, hardworking Hannibal Ray gave no more thought for tomorrow than Mac ever did.

Unlike Mac, Hannibal always landed on his feet. Landing on his feet despite whatever obstacles came his way commanded respect from the men and women of Half Dead, Texas.

Mac envied his nemesis and the free way he lived, without people shaking their heads in disappointment the way they shook their heads and said things about him such as, "He could have been somebody," or, "What a waste."

Instead of ridiculing him, Mac knew that when people spotted Hannibal moving through town they said, "Wonder where he's going now," or, "Wish I was him." For the wonderers in Half Dead, Hannibal had been, and probably would always be, the ultimate adventurer.

Most days were an adventure for Hannibal because he rarely planned beyond the moment. Anyone who knew him seldom expected much from him because he had very little to give other than his name and his honor. For those two reasons, he risked his all every day, something Mac had known about Hannibal ever since they were kids.

Because of their childhood bond, a bond centered around their desire to fight each other, a desire neither of them could explain, Mac knew Hannibal believed that without his good name and his honor, he was nobody.

Keeping the two qualities of name and honor intact created a challenge for Hannibal; over the years, that challenge became a strength for him to build on, an obstacle for Mac to try to knock down.

On this Sunday afternoon, the challenge for Hannibal was as simple as facing off with another man in an old-fashioned fistfight—no guns, no knives, no outside help from the gathering crowd, just true iron-man grit, blue-collar gumption.

Mac wanted to beat Hannibal so badly he

stopped hearing the crowd egging them on. He stopped seeing the crowd at all. Just once he wanted to knock Hannibal flat.

In his whole miserable life Mac had never been able to do even that small thing, which was the reason their fighting drew spectators each time the men faced off in a test of their physical strength.

The circle of half-drunk men and women spurred the two enemies on. The voices of the crowd went from quiet betting to hoots and hollers for more than the bruising of flesh; they wanted the breaking of bones.

These spectators were people who wanted something to *do*. They wanted an event to show them they were alive after all, that the afternoon they were living was not a carbon copy of the same afternoon that had just passed them by.

Hannibal heard all the shouting; he welcomed it. He catered to all the perverse calls for more, more, more with fancy foot moves, head bobbing and body weaving. A natural athlete in his prime, he was a grand-slam show of physical prowess——until Mac Bishop did the unthinkable. Mac knocked Hannibal down, flat on his back, with a sucker punch that left him lying on the ground feeling dazed.

Mac stood over his nemesis and felt awed that he had laid him flat on his back. Mac stared at his fists as if they belonged to some other man. When the reality of the moment, the absolute rarity of his success sank into his mind, he let out a roar filled with triumph. In an instant, Mac Bishop had become a hero, and Hannibal Ray had become the laughing-stock of Half Dead.

A spectator lifted Hannibal from the ground onto his spit-damp, tobacco-stained boots. His ears rang with the sound of ribald laughter over Mac's surprise victory, a triumph which set the gloating man in a strut within the win-ning circle of half-drunk men and women.

Mac's success was the puff behind his chest, the sucking in of his gut, the spouting of in-sults in the general direction of the beaten man. Soon, he would need ice to cover the bruises on his hands and the swelling on his face, but Mac cared nothing about that now; at long last, it was his turn to shine.

Hannibal hated the way Mac bragged and paraded around with his new pride. Worse, he hated the speculative looks in the eyes of his former fans. Hannibal imagined he could feel their thoughts, hear them whispering between themselves: "Has Hannibal lost his edge? Has he lost his nerve?"

Hannibal scanned the whispering crowd. He bet they figured that if the unthinkable could happen to him, the unthinkable could happen to any one of them too. This bracing thought reminded Hannibal how very average he and the crowd were that Sunday afternoon, average and jaded.

He decided to fight again only if the fight was for a good reason such as the preservation of honor, justice, or beauty. His fight with Mac Bishop had been for none of those three reasons. For the first time in a long time, Hannibal Ray felt ashamed of himself.

He took stock of his surroundings. It was a pretty blue Sunday afternoon. Instead of spending the day with their families, the crowd still pressed around him spent the day in front of a worn-out bar begging men to fight for a two-dollar bet.

The women who watched the surprise ending of the fifteen-minute fight lingered a while longer than the men. Their avid eyes were intent now upon the town underdog, Mac Bishop, Half Dead's new and best hero.

For a short while, the women forgot that with little exception, Mac was no prize as a human being. He had the nasty habit of fathering children with no real thought of being a dad.

For a few magic moments the women forgot Mac really was a loser in life. The women forgot that even though Hannibal made them few promises, he had always been kind to them; he had always been a fair and reliable friend.

The novelty of Mac's win led the women to join the men in their exodus for more beer inside the rickety bar. They too wanted to be in on the juicy gossip needed to turn a common fight between common men into the stuff of small-town legend.

More outdone by the instant betrayal of his former fans than by the sucker punch from Mac, Hannibal did something no one in Half Dead had the nerve to do.

He took the clothes on his back, the wallet in his butt pocket, the hat on his head, and left town with no more thought for tomorrow than a wild buck in the Texas woods.

Those people who lingered after the fight saw his grand exit. The grim look on his face told them all to keep their distance and their gossiping mouths shut.

Only one woman broke the stiff silence of the few lingerers who liked Hannibal the man, not just Hannibal the fighter. That woman was Rosalie Jones, ex-prom queen, mother of three, wife to no one. Rosalie was stout-hearted, fine-natured, as durable as the town of Half Dead.

"Hannibal Ray!" she screamed, her white apron flapping in the breeze. "Wait!"

He turned slowly, his muscles already pounding with pain, his battered face already sore. Despite the way his body hurt, Hannibal's spirit stirred with a fresh quest to venture into the unknown.

He was long overdue to leave Half Dead, and way too old to be fighting a grown man for nothing, but he stopped to speak to Rosalie. She deserved at least that much from him. He said, "What for?"

"Me."

He thought of her children, of the single-wide trailer she lived in alone, of the lily pond he built for her the summer before in a water barrel bleached gray by the withering rays of the sun. She would always be a special friend to him.

He knew what she was asking, the same question he had asked himself a hundred times in the years he had known her. The question had everything to do with marriage, a thing he had vowed never to do. He gazed down at her with regret. "I'm not the marrying kind."

"Don't go."

"You deserve more than I am, Rosalie."

She reached out to him, her hands chapped from washing dishes and cleaning tables. Her rough fingers were poised to clutch his arm, to hold on to him always, but she stopped short of doing it; she was too proud to beg.

In the end, she used her ringless fingers to smooth down the flying hem of her white cotton apron, on loan from Bob Otto's Famous Smoked Ribs, the wood building that leaned to the left behind her.

"It's not the kids, Rosalie."

"I know."

He walked away from her then. Carefully, he folded his bruised body into the cab of his faded silver truck. The few possessions he owned were in a box on the truck bed, as if premonition had warned him that this day might be his last in a town where every man knew his name.

Hannibal left Half Dead without glancing back. He left Rosalie in tears, and he knew he had done, for them both, the right thing. What woman would have him, a man incapable of loving long or deeply, a man who sometimes needed to be alone to feel strong?

Hannibal drove into the great unknown, the gas tank in his one-ton Chevy on full, his banged-up heart on empty because he knew exactly why it was that Rosalie cried.

She cried because he had used her. Despite repairing her home, spending time with her children, making love to her any way she wanted to make love for however short or long she needed it, he had used her simply to pass the summer months, which was the very reason he felt like a bastard.

She had been courted, finessed, then ultimately betrayed by a man who failed to give her the love she deserved because he failed to love himself completely.

He failed to love himself completely because he felt something significant was missing in his life, something that made him feel incomplete. But what?

He wished he knew.

Hannibal drove on, his soul cold even as wanderlust set his mind on fire.

Rosalie Jones could never hold him.

No woman could.

TWO

Josephine Brennon told herself for the umpteenth time that her little world really was lovely, that there was nothing else she needed to do to her home that would make it a better place to live.

The rare social guests who came to her home often asked her to consider revamping her yellow and white farmhouse by turning it into a quaint bed-and-breakfast.

No matter how many people told Josephine that being in her home was like being in heaven's own paradise, she had a hard time believing their words to be true, no matter how genuine those words sounded.

She rarely believed the kind words because to her, a real paradise was a place to roam free, a place where weary souls came to rest from obstacles and despair. In Josephine's tiny world, there was one major obstacle, one source of despair: fear.

Fear held her captive, a prisoner in her own home. At twenty-five years old, she was afraid to open the gate to her white picket fence. As long as she stayed behind the fence, her destiny was a known thing, a comfortable thing. She was bored half to death.

She was also a coward. Josephine cared so much about what people said about her, how people treated her, that she stayed at home—safe, undisturbed, and lonely.

So she changed her home constantly. Through mail-order catalogs and an intricate barter system with town residents, she had created a private space so unique she could almost believe that where she lived truly was as original as Eden.

But then she would look beyond the weathered white gate to her front yard. When she looked beyond that hand-built border, she would see the same thing she saw every day—Destiny.

Destiny was a small town, an eccentric town, a town where carriages drawn with horses traveled the same path as four-wheel drives, pickups, and Cadillacs.

It was a place of renewal, where crumbling brick buildings had grown so old, their appeal had gone full circle to gain fresh value as sources of potential future posterity. Destiny was fast becoming a tourist town.

Tourism meant outsiders, people who rarely knew the names of their neighbors, rarely knew their neighbors' personal histories, the kind of facts that separated the do-gooders from the people with real heart.

It was because of her name, her heart, and her history that Josephine was able to thrive in Destiny without ever having to leave her sprawling front yard.

In small towns like hers, people took care of their own, took care of them despite damning secrets, shady business deals, or deeds so dirty it sometimes took leading citizens to keep those dirty deeds hushed.

The residents of Destiny were kind to each other because being kind was their best way of getting along. It was their best way of getting along because town residents shopped at the same grocery stores, bought gas from the same quick stops, ate food off the same tables in eateries run by mutual relatives, mutual friends, mutual acquaintances.

A person could do wrong in Destiny, could even run away from outrageous troubles in Destiny, but no one, not one single person could flat-out hide in a town of 15,000 residents.

This single fact—not being able to hide— was the source of the town's eccentricity. The hot-white light of criticism forced the residents to be kind when the last thing anybody wanted to be was kind.

Being kind was tough when a crime had been committed, such as a woman in her twenties being too terrified to walk away from her own house. Being kind, Josephine had found, was all about existing in harmony with her surroundings, which is exactly what she did, one day after another, every day of her life.

She left nothing to chance. Living this way, one hour at a time, helped her to survive. However, despite her well-constructed peace, Josephine was very, very restless, and so desperately alone.

She did what she always did when she felt restless. She stepped one foot in front of the other until she reached her kitchen with its gleaming steel stove and cream-tiled countertops.

From her kitchen, she made food for the elderly and for the homeless. The food was bought and distributed through a charity organization within the Good Faith Baptist Church, Reverend Franklin's church.

In truth she was a cook who specialized in nothing fancy, just honest, basic food—healing food. Selling food to the church paid her bills. It was a monotonous life, every day the same, like insects marching.

Around her, beyond the gate to her paradise, was a homestead composed of six acres, a two-story wood home, a small shed converted into a cottage, and two gardens: one for vegetables, the other for flowers. There were a few farm animals she kept as pets, two cows and some chickens.

On the distant border of her property there was a wind-damaged fence that needed new posts as well as entire six-by-eight foot sections of new wood.

Dead limbs from one of the oak trees needed splitting for winter fires. An old outhouse needed tearing down and hauling away. The lawn needed reseeding. Shingles dangled from the roof. A second-floor window of the turn-of-the century Victorian farmhouse was cracked.

Josephine's home needed the strong hands of a man and she needed that man's tender loving; but what man in his right mind would take on a woman so afraid to step beyond her front yard that day after day, without fail, she had to be sure the gate on her white picket fence was locked?

Knowing she would never find such a man was the prime source of Josephine Brennon's discontent. Without her own very special man there would be no children, no one to curl up with her before a winter fire.

No man could love a needy, lonely woman like her.

A desperate woman.

Or so she thought.

THREE

Early January
Destiny, Oklahoma
Sunday

Hannibal hated to admit it, but he was exhausted. A month of living on the road, sometimes sleeping in his truck at rest stops, had taken a physical and mental toll on him.

It was damp outside. The lukewarm weather of early December had given way to the chill of colder weather. His well-used sheepskin coat was warm, but not warm enough for the coming storms of winter.

It was time for him to settle down someplace until spring. He had been sleeping in his truck to save money so he could one day stay in a room that was clean and decent. Meanwhile, he took on odd jobs to keep his truck's tank and his stomach on full.

He eased off Interstate 35 into Destiny, a town where no man knew his name. He was after shelter, strictly basic, enough food to keep him satisfied, and the company of new friends for the long winter nights ahead. The challenge to acquire these things banked the fires of Hannibal's wanderlust, however briefly.

His silver Chevy rumbled into Destiny with zero fanfare. Trucks dirty with red road dust were nothing to marvel at in a town where farmers and ranchers rubbed elbows with doctors and bankers.

From Stetson to boots, he fit right in with the rest of the small town. The light weight of his wallet pressed between his right hip and the ripped tweed of his bench seat. It was the half-empty state of his wallet that prompted his next adventure: to find a job among strangers.

To find a job, he needed the classifieds. After a stop at a convenience store to buy a thin daily newspaper, he focused his thoughts on the next pressing matter: food. He took the newspaper to Fat Willie's, a fast-food grill specializing in onion burgers.

It was quiet at Fat Willie's, so he had his pick of empty tables. He chose a table with a view of Main Street. Using a dot of ketchup from the bottle on the square table, he marked an ad for a general handyman, lodging included, at a home somewhere in the mansion-filled town.

His meal finished, Hannibal searched out the street address. He felt a strange jolt of recognition, as if somehow or another he had been led to this small Victorian-styled town.

It was a restless thought, and Hannibal did not believe in fate. He believed a man made his mark in the world by upholding justice, by doing the right things at the right times and for the right reasons. His code of living had been fine until the day he left Rosalie Jones behind. It was the same day he realized it was time to make his stamp on the world. At the very least, it was time to find out why he felt so incomplete.

It rankled him that he had yet to leave his personal mark, the kind of imprint that made a lasting change in a troubled person's life. Before he died, Hannibal's daddy had told him that a real man separated himself from the losers only after he championed someone less powerful than himself.

Hannibal's carefree style of living set him at odds with his daddy's way of thinking. It took time and patience to select and befriend someone in need of a defender.

With great care, Hannibal had built a life with no attachments. He was homeless by choice, single by design, connected to nothing and no one in particular because he chose not to be tied down. He cared only about the day in which he lived—the only day he was promised.

He was sorry about one thing: Never had he been someone's hero. In this way, he had let his daddy down.

In all his adventures, Hannibal made sure

he used his strength to defend, not conquer. When he fought with Mac, it was more a game of strength than a true desire to hurt his opponent or to destroy him.

Because he kept to himself, a habit formed by a life spent rambling, Hannibal was a shadow of the man he could be, a mere fifty percent of his full potential.

He seldom stayed in a single place long enough to make a serious statement about his worth as a man. Because he moved often, he gave himself little time to be content, not even for love.

Rosalie had loved him and he had left her. Homeowner and mother of three, Rosalie had been, to him, a hero in her own right. Through her dedication to living a good life within her means, to raising her children to be strong, she had left her mark in the world.

This mark of hers was a brand on Hannibal's conscience. The brand reminded him that no matter how hard he tried, he could not love Rosalie the way she deserved to be loved, with all his heart and mind. His life was in limbo, a feeling he fought by wandering.

Wandering took him up and down the middle of the country. He roamed with the hope that somewhere in his travels there might be a place or a person so special, his need to wander would disappear.

In truth, Hannibal was tired of having no

home to call his own. He was tired of being alone.

The directions listed in the ad were easy for him to follow. He found the street address he needed, a seven-minute ride from Fat Willie's. To his surprise he discovered a charming farmhouse. There were neighboring homes in sight, all of them out of shouting range of the house itself.

An aura of comfort embraced the old wood building. The subtle cheer of the home revived him, even as the hamburger lunch combo eased his hunger, and the ad for the handyman job gave him hope.

With subconscious thought, his gaze pinned to the beauty before him, Hannibal threw the truck's engine into park. He unlatched the belt of his seat, left his paper-scattered cab, and opened the gate to a three-foot-high white picket fence.

The fence bordered a yard where the grass was still bright green. Against a white gingerbread porch rail was a yellow rambling rose, half a dozen flowers in striking bloom.

As Hannibal made his approach up the stone walk, his feet crunched against the fallen dry leaves of huge sycamore trees. Above him, heavy lace at a second-floor window, its stained glass cracked from time or rock or weather, parted slightly as if the watcher from the window wanted to see and not be seen in return. The idiosyncrasy of the secret viewer marched Hannibal up the steps to the front door, his mind filled with anticipation. He waited a full three minutes for someone to welcome him beyond the painted door into the home which seemed to beckon him.

At five o'clock in the afternoon it was near dark, the moon a sacred symbol in a slate-colored sky. In the distance, a train blared its horn. The increasing wind kicked grit against Hannibal's face, yet the oddest feeling washed over him as he shoved his hands into the tight pockets of his favorite Lee jeans.

There, in the growing winter cold, on a peeling white porch draped in roses so fine they were picture perfect, in a town where tractors shared Main Street with privately owned big rigs, Hannibal Ray felt as if he had come home.

FOUR

Josephine Brennon hired the tall stranger on the spot. She conducted her business with him inside the space of four minutes, he standing on her threshold, she facing him.

At the start of the third minute, she took another detailed look at her new handyman. She did it slowly, as if engraving a permanent image of him on her mind.

What she saw was a cowboy straight out of a Marlboro tobacco ad, a man who wore Lee jeans, tan leather boots thick with road dust, and a Stetson he probably slept in.

The cowboy's skin was dark as rum, his hands big, the fingers long. Despite the dust that followed him, the nails on his fingers were clean and neatly clipped.

Josephine could tell a lot by looking at a man's hands, and she had the feeling that this man's hands were kind. It was because of the kindness she saw in his hands that she hired him.

She spoke in a voice made husky because

she had not used it to speak with anyone all day, not even on the telephone. "You'll do."

He was strangely flattered. This was the first time anyone had hired him on face value, no questions asked. For a woman to extend this first act of good faith was an experience that uplifted Hannibal, as the yellow climbing roses had uplifted him when he first saw them in bloom on the porch of the Brennon Victorian farmhouse.

He had heard of roses blooming in winter, only he had never seen one until now. It was a beautiful sight that pleased him as much as the owner of the house pleased him by granting him entrance into such a paradise. "I suppose you want to know where I came from," he offered, his voice an easy, soothing drawl designed to keep any fear she felt at bay.

Despite her eager response to his answering of the newspaper ad for a handyman, he believed she had to have some sort of qualm or two about hiring him so quickly.

He was a full-grown man, with a full-grown man's wants and desires. She was young, physically fit, and no one in Destiny knew he had been invited into her home.

Despite the bold once-over she had given him during his four-minute interview, Hannibal could tell she was scared; a muscle twitched beneath her right eye.

She shrugged. "It doesn't matter where you came from. It only matters that you're here."

Her response was so unexpected, he could not think of a thing to say. He pulled his Stetson off his head to reveal a short, neat haircut. He crushed the hat between his fingers.

Josephine was not scared of the new arrival; she was excited. Opening the front door to her home completely, she let him in.

He stifled a whistle. The house was as big as it looked from the outside. The foyer, simply decorated with live ficus trees rooted in terracotta flowerpots, was large enough to hold a king-sized bed.

Carved wood molding fit the corners of the vaulted ceiling. The main room had been decorated with antique furniture, although the walls held framed modern art. The fireplace was lit. Hannibal felt like pinching himself at the unexpected beauty of it all. What was he doing here? And why did it feel so right?

His feelings on edge, he said as mildly as he could muster, "Nice place you've got here."

"Thank you."

She showed him where he would sleep, not in the farmhouse with her, but in the tiny building behind the house, at the end of the cobblestone kitchen walk, its edges lined with monkey grass, its slender stems of lavender flowers long since out of bloom.

It was a rustic dwelling, painted white to match the trim on the farmhouse. An herb garden, which still had red geraniums in bloom, served as the focal point of the quaint little cottage.

When they brushed by the spearmint in clay pots at either side of the wood door, the scent of something fresh and new perfumed the air. To Hannibal, it smelled like hope.

He had expected to find a job doing manual labor, making just enough money to rent a room in a small hotel or boarding house. He never expected to meet someone like Josephine, a definite risk taker despite her soft manner and husky voice. He might have lived for the moment, but this woman took the cake.

"You live alone," he stated, suddenly a bit uneasy.

He did not bother to hide his surprise. In a house as friendly as this one, he expected to find children's toys scattered in the backyard, a swing. Instead he saw only beauty, nothing fun, nothing haphazard.

The scene was so perfect he might have been inside a postcard or travel guide filled with photos of rural southern towns. Nothing, Hannibal reasoned, could be this good.

Calm as still water, she flipped on the light inside his new home before saying, "Of course."

Hannibal was so outdone by her cavalier attitude, he scarcely noticed the cottage she showed him. The eight hundred square-foot dwelling had two windows, a full bath, a short refrigerator, but no kitchen.

He did notice the cherry wood dresser with the brass candleholders and dark green candles on top. He saw the heavy brass bed with its curlicue headboard, a bed big enough to fit in the foyer at the house.

He even noticed the wedding ring quilt on the bed. However, he did not spare those details more than a passing thought. His mind was focused on two words: "Of course."

Josephine's cryptic answer worked like the dot of ketchup from the fast food restaurant on the daily newspaper that had led him to her front door in the first place.

The flip answer to his question marked her place in his mind, a new territory to explore. His boss was a contradiction he found appealing; she was nervous yet brave, cautious yet decisive, young yet strong. Why else would he be standing where he was, a stranger in such paradise?

He could not believe his luck. When it got down to it, he could not believe Josephine. He all but stared at her with his mouth hanging open.

"Of course," she had said. Was she really that accustomed to strange men in her house?

He thought of the twitch beneath her eye and did not think so. But how could he tell when he did not know her? Maybe he had been wrong about the fear he first sensed in her. Certainly something was wrong about this scenario, but what?

She lived alone in a house big enough for a family of ten people, a dog, and two cats. She had enough land to need a tractor to mow it. She had enough nerve to hire him without asking for references. He wanted to ask her if she was crazy, but he needed the job.

Hannibal was so busy thinking about what made Josephine tick, she had to repeat herself.

"Supper," she said again, her voice still husky from infrequent use, "will be ready at seven."

His gaze took her in with wonder. She was not a big woman. She could not have been more than five feet five inches tall, a hundred and twenty pounds. She could have taken a course in self-defense, but still, she should not have interviewed him alone—if you could call snap judgment an interview.

She should be wary, at least ask him where he came from, do something more than stare with fixed concentration at the nails of his long fingers and the knuckles of his big, calloused hands.

If she was afraid of something, it sure was not him. Hannibal could not help it. He was flabbergasted. He had to ask, "You really aren't scared to take me on, are you?"

There it was again, that cavalier, don't-give-a-damn shrug that was so at odds with the cultivated beauty around him. This time, Josephine not only shrugged, she lifted her left brow.

It was a long and slender brow, and it had not been plucked. Hannibal could not believe he had noticed such a thing. He could not even remember Rosalie's eyebrows, let alone if she plucked them.

To her credit, Josephine did not bother to pretend she had no clue what he was talking about. "Should I be scared?" she asked.

"No."

She had the nerve to turn her back on him. Hannibal, his mouth open for real this time, had been dismissed. He should not have been surprised by her actions. After all, she was the boss, not his lover.

As his boss, she had already shown him that she was a decision maker and not someone who straddled the fence of dos and don'ts. If he turned out to be bad news, she would have no one to blame for her fast decision to hire him but herself.

She had no reason to tell him good-bye, but he wished she had. If she had said good-bye, he would feel that things would eventually progress as business as usual. So far, from the flowers in bloom out of season to the way he had been hired, nothing was business as usual. Not one thing.

He watched her leave, a funny feeling fluttering through his chest. She moved as if she owned time. She moved as if time worked solely for her.

She walked briskly, with nothing sexy thrown

into it, yet she seemed to maximize every second of the effort to get from his cottage to the house where she lived alone.

Alone.

How dare she not ask his name?

Instead, she had stared at his hands, touched them with a wise woman's eyes that made him think of home and hearth and the kind of food that filled a man up without making him wish for something sweet when he was done, something extra on the side.

He watched her open the kitchen door to her picturebook house and close it without checking behind her to see if he followed. He figured this was strange behavior for a woman living alone, and still, this was not the cause for the flutter of his heart.

His heart fluttered in response to the deep scar that stretched from her left cheekbone to her chin. This woman who lived alone, a woman who had hired him by some secret code of trust he was not privy to, made his fighting man's hands itch to hit somebody.

Born with wanderlust, seasoned by a life roaming from one odd job to another between south Texas and the Dakotas, Hannibal knew a cattle brand when he saw one.

Josephine Brennon, his twenty-something and very mysterious new boss, had been branded with the letter X.

FIVE

Back in her kitchen, Josephine prepared dinner for her guest. She started the meal with the chicken she had bartered from a neighbor that morning for a bushel of turnip greens.

With an economy of motion based on practiced skill, she cut the fresh fowl into serving-sized pieces with a stainless-steel meat cleaver she pulled from the drawer where she kept the sharpest of her cooking knives.

She secured all-purpose flour from a tin in the cupboard. To the flour she added only enough salt and pepper to bring out the full taste of her elderly neighbor's fat chicken.

While the oil came to just the right heat in the cast-iron skillet her Aunt Cordelia once used, she dredged the cleaned meat in the seasoned flour until it was coated on all sides.

Once the seasoned meat had browned in the hot skillet, she drained off some of the excess fat. She added flour to the remaining fat with enough milk to make gravy.

As the meat simmered, she cleared the

kitchen counter of dirty dishes, then set to work on the buttermilk biscuits. The biscuits came from the oven big and round and ready for butter if the hired hand wanted some.

When the meal finished cooking, she spooned it into blue crockery, which she put on the pine table in her dining room. The fine cotton linen she used to dress the table had been passed down to her from two generations of Brennon women.

Stepping away from the table, Josephine felt no fear. She was in her element, and wanted to share this part of her complicated life with the man who had come to her from a place she would never know. It was a huge risk, taking a strange man into her home. The risk thrilled her.

The suspense of the near, uncertain future stirred her hidden feelings in a subtle, exquisite way. Anticipation, the best thrill of all, raced its way through her body from foot to thigh, hip to breast, shoulder to brow.

Never in all her life would Josephine have pictured a man so rugged and virile sharing a meal with her, especially food served within the comfort and complete solitude of her big old Victorian home.

The sharing of food was a big deal to Josephine. Food was her gift to the world, her thanks to God for the chance to be alive; and perhaps, if she dared to believe, it was He who had delivered Hannibal into Destiny, into her very own paradise.

Waiting for her mystery man to knock on the kitchen door for his supper, Josephine was almost sorry he would never know how pleased she was to have him dine at her table. He was a welcome respite from the monotony of the coming winter days.

Seeing that she could use help to manage her aging property, many men in town had offered to repair her home for a small price. Had she hired one of those local men, there would have been no need to include food or lodging as payment for services rendered.

Yet something had compelled her to place the ad in the daily newspaper, her mood restless at the time she had ordered the classified ad by telephone. When she placed that ad, her energy had been at the lowest ebb of her life.

Somehow, what she had done, all but asking flat out for the help of a stranger, felt right. Now that Hannibal was here, she was more than glad, she was happy, and she would use food to tell him so.

In her bedroom, she removed her casual cotton dress quickly in order to put on a chocolate brown sweater over an ankle-length skirt. The flowers in the skirt had faded from too many washes, yet the skirt was soft because of them.

As she dressed, she thought again of the rum-colored drifter, of his snug jeans, cracked boots, and eyes so bold she was sure they had not missed one thing about her.

Simply thinking of those bold, dark eyes caused Josephine to carry a tentative hand to her left cheek, briefly, and then the hand fell away from the damaged flesh to stroke the rich brown of her hair.

Her hair. Yes, it was still in place. The wiry ponytail that fell below her shoulder blades was still bound fast with a red rubber band. The band was as tight as her wish to be lovely in a kind man's eyes, a wish she did not believe would come true, not even for a little while.

Standing in the mirror, her mind taking stock of her own reflection, Josephine clinically examined her physical measurements. She was five feet five inches tall, weighed 125 pounds, and wore a size six. Her skin was the color of pecan shells, crushed fine, her eyes a darker shade of brown, the color she favored most in her wardrobe.

There was nothing special she saw in her own reflection, nothing special at all, and yet, on this night, it mattered little what she wore or even that her face was badly scarred. She had company, by God, and tonight, her company was all that mattered.

It was terribly important to Josephine that her dinner guest be made to feel welcome. If food was her gift to the world, then her home was her gift to herself.

On this early winter night, she would have the opportunity to share both of the things she loved with a man who looked as if he had spent two full days in the clothes he wore on his back.

The man was a drifter, an urban nomad, the kind of man who did whatever he wanted to do whenever he wanted to do it. She imagined that a man who laid his hat wherever he damn well pleased was also the kind of man who set his own rules, played his own games.

She liked that kind of independence; that kind of freedom took self-confidence and sheer guts. If his independence made him dangerous, well then, she liked the danger, too.

Because of his drifting, she viewed her new handyman as an open book, and if he was an open book, then he was also a breath of fresh air. Open books had no secrets; open books were meant to be read.

Josephine wanted to read this particular book from cover to cover, beginning with the stranger's name. Not knowing his name created an element of suspense, a component she lacked in her reclusive life.

Oblivious to the stark pleasure in her deep brown eyes, she twirled away from her reflection in the polished glass of her bedroom mirror. She left the second-floor bedroom to join her dinner guest, her movements brisk, the sound of her booted feet against the smooth floors in tune with the swift rhythm of her heart.

Tonight—her breath quickened at the thought—tonight she would not be alone. To punctuate this quiet joy, Josephine Brennon added spiced peaches to her dinner table for dessert.

SIX

The Brennon Farmhouse
7:00 PM

Proper introductions made, Hannibal found himself seated at Josephine's table. In a silence that was friendly, he felt the knots of tension between his shoulder blades relax. Until now, he had not been sure of his decision to stay. Chivalry was one thing, common sense something else.

It angered him that Josephine had been hurt by another human being. Common sense told him it no longer mattered who had put that terrible scar on her face, there was nothing he could do about it now. The damage to her skin had been done. To his great regret, he was too late to be her hero.

Hannibal began his relationship with her the same way he began with every significant woman in his life, business or personal. He opened his speech with a one-liner that varied only slightly to suit the occasion.

"I'll stay until the repairs you need are done."

His voice was so deep, it shimmied straight over her skin. Josephine wanted to ask him why he felt the need to clarify his intentions toward her, but all she said was, "Fine."

For the first time in a long time, Hannibal found himself with a woman who talked less than he did. Rosalie would have felt pressured to keep their words alive. Either Josephine was entirely self-contained or she felt she had nothing of value to say.

As he watched, she filled her mouth with food, then savored it against her tongue, as if she separated the taste of the pepper from the salt, the gravy from the meat. Her absolute calm unnerved him.

He was a stranger and yet she behaved without caution around him. The fluttering of his heart reminded Hannibal that hurting Josephine was a thing he could never do. In the end, it was he who reached out to her, this troubled woman who touched his heart. He chose a subject he sensed was a source of her pride.

"Supper was great."

"Thank you."

He patted his stomach, the muscles flat from working in fields harvesting hay and from branding cattle. His tone easy and soft, he said, "It's been a long time since I had a down-home meal that tastes as good as yours."

She smiled.

It was a small smile, a delighted smile. The sight of this quiet joy pleased him so much Hannibal found himself saying, "When I was little and my grandmother pickled peaches, I'd sit on her back porch with my brothers and eat a whole jar."

This time it was her eyes that lit up, the glow in them as soft as her smile had been. It seemed suddenly important to him that her smile be wide instead of small.

All dressed in brown the way she was, he wondered if anyone cared enough about Josephine to see to her happiness, to make sure she laughed out loud sometimes, had fun with her friends. He thought of her hiring him without asking for references, without asking his name and knew that it was he who was in trouble, not she.

Josephine Brennon was untapped depths of emotion, a woman with a past so vicious, she carried its mark against her cheek. The heavy-handed brand drew Hannibal to her as surely as the scent of the food that had lured him to her kitchen.

Crazy and unexpected as it was, he wanted to . . . lay down with her, in the room right above them, the room where the lace curtains were drawn against the crack in the window.

He had no business thinking what he was thinking, but being rational was the last thing on his mind. He wanted to make love to a woman he had no idea even existed until this day.

He might feel crazy right now, but it was a craziness he understood. Something about the woman who sat across from him felt one-hundred percent right, the very way he had felt when he saw her ad in the classified section of the daily local newspaper.

It was this same sense of rightness which made him feel as if he had come home when he stood on the front porch near the yellow roses in bloom. It was not an intuition that he tried to analyze, it was a state of feeling he took at face value, in the same way Josephine had taken him at face value.

As Josephine had done in the mirror of her bedroom, Hannibal did now, in the quiet comfort of Josephine's kitchen; he took stock. Only there was no mirrored reflection for him to study, there was only a view to interpret—his point of view.

There was the food, which of course was delicious. As his grandmother would say, she had put her foot in it, which meant the food was not just excellent but beyond compare. The home itself was at least a century old, isolated, its owner young and seemingly alone.

If there was an element of menace inside this closed setting, then the menace was whatever caused her to hide out in the first place. He did not need anyone to tell him that his new boss seldom left her home. The evidence was in every room he had seen so far.

In the living room, there was a television, but no radio. On the shelves there were hundreds of books. On a side table were at least thirty mail-order catalogs.

In the kitchen on a small portable wood table was a twelve-inch television set. On a shelf below the television set were more mail-order catalogs. In the driveway, there was no car. There were no horses.

"You shouldn't have hired me, Josephine."

His voice was heavy with sorrow, for himself as well as for her. Even if she would have him in her bed, he was a drifter. Drifters never stayed in one place for long.

Her smile never changed. It was her eyes he could not read. In her eyes there was no past, no future. Her pupils were dark brown, beyond chocolate, the mind behind them closed to his view. She made her question sound like an absurdity. "Are you a criminal?"

"No."

"Did you run away from your responsibilities?"

He thought of Rosalie, and was glad he had made no promises to her for a future sealed with a wedding ring. For this reason, he said without regret, "If you mean a wife and kids, no."

With mystery in her eyes, she measured the power in his hands. Slowly, all the time in the world on her side, Josephine smiled until her whole face lit up.

His heart stuttered, then stopped completely. The brightness of Josephine's smile transformed her face, the freshness of it erasing from Hannibal's mind the scar engraved on her left cheek.

Her smile drew him to her with the promise of a thousand secret pleasures. She leaned across the supper table to touch one knuckle of his hand with the tip of an index finger. His heart roared into life again.

"I believe," she said cryptically, her real thoughts still closed to him, "I chose well."

Before he could get a fix on his feelings and form a reply, somebody crashed the dinner party.

It was eight o'clock, full dark outside, the moon huge in a sky thick with stars. There were no hills or tall buildings to break Josephine's view when she answered the hard knocking on her front door. There was only her last living relative, her mother's sister, Cordelia Brennon.

"Why didn't you tell me you were smothering chicken?" Cordelia demanded. Annoyed by the lack of information, she brushed by her niece without a kind word. "Girl, you know smothered chicken is my favorite thing to eat."

Accustomed to her aunt's rude ways, Josephine studied her elder with practiced calm. At sixty, Cordelia was five feet seven inches tall.

Her hair, worn in short pressed curls, was gray at the temples. Her eyes were small, the lashes on them short. She wore no makeup.

Her skin was flawless, as if it was too stubborn to yield to the aging effects of the sun. Time had not stamped the mark of wisdom on Cordelia's face; it had stamped the bitterness of old grudges in the form of lines around a pinched mouth.

"I've been busy," Josephine said.

She looked at the fine lines around her aunt's mouth and felt restless. Why couldn't her aunt just leave her alone? She knew why Cordelia came to her home without an invitation, for the same reason her lips were pinched right now: Cordelia hated what Josephine stood for, her own lost innocence. Cordelia muscled her way into the mellow glow of the nook in the kitchen, but stopped mid–stride when she saw Hannibal. As a sign of respect, he stood from the table.

Her suspicious eyes roving, Cordelia put her hands on her hips. "So what do we have here?"

Josephine resumed her seat. She was pleased with the thunderstruck look on Cordelia's face. It was not often her aunt was speechless. "Aunt Cordelia, meet Hannibal Ray. He's my new handyman."

Cordelia declined Hannibal's hand, ignored his deep-spoken hello. She pulled a chair away from the pine table so that it was she who sat

at its head. Her body filled the ladderback
chair. Her thighs spread to make room for her
stomach.

She inspected Josephine's guest with beady
black eyes. He was clean and polite, too good-
looking a stranger to be alone with her niece.
Had she not stopped by for a visit, she would
have missed seeing him altogether. "Did you
say candyman?" she asked.

Hannibal laughed.

Josephine wanted to laugh, but she did not
dare. Her aunt was ticked off enough. "No,
Aunt Cordelia. I said 'handyman.' "

For the first time since barging into Josephine's home, Cordelia took stock of the scene
around her. The smothered chicken was gone.
One biscuit was visible from under a linen
napkin in a small honey-colored bread basket.
What was left of the vegetables could only be
considered a snack.

She heard the hum of the refrigerator, the
slow drip of the kitchen faucet into the sink,
the sound of logs crackling in the stone fireplace on the north wall of the living room.

She heard the wind begin to howl in ear-
nest, the way she wanted to howl in shock and
dismay over the peace she had interrupted.
Peace was something she did not have at home
or in herself.

Her niece was alone with a gorgeous man,
a man who looked totally sated with good food
and fine company. Unlike her, Hannibal Ray

had no need to venture out into the cold, dark night with its full moon and howling wind.

He did not have to go to his bed knowing he had crashed an intimate moment between a man and a woman who were content with each other until an outsider arrived. She could not stand to see so much quiet fun and know she would never be part of it.

She said with spite, "The good reverend is gonna hear about this." She placed her scratched patent leather pocketbook on the table. "Handyman my foot."

Hannibal raised a brow over her grumbling. Wisely, he kept his thoughts to himself.

Josephine enjoyed the way he went with the flow of things. He did not leave the room so that she had to deal with her aunt's rudeness by herself. Unlike Cordelia, she had invited him to her table. Josephine stared at his hands. Strangely, she felt safe.

Cordelia sniffed the air as if to catch the fresh scent of sex instead of the spiced peaches her niece had served for dessert. "The reverend won't like this at all."

"I've got nothing to hide, Aunt Cordelia. I put an ad for a handyman in the local paper."

Despite Josephine's neutral tone, Cordelia detected apprehension. She felt smug to think that one of her barbs had penetrated the younger woman's confidence.

"I saw the ad. Didn't think you'd gone this crazy though." She humphed. "I can't believe that with all the stray men in this town, you had to go off and hire somebody don't nobody know."

Josephine tried to appear oblivious to her aunt's barbs that she and her guest were doing something illicit. She gathered the soiled linen napkins from the table.

"Then you shouldn't be surprised about seeing Hannibal," she quietly fought back. She reminded herself she was grown. She had done nothing wrong.

Cordelia huffed. She could not get over Josephine's spunk, a woman who was traditionally reserved, a hermit even, a woman no man wanted because her face was scarred.

"Don't get smart with me, girl. I'll tell the reverend."

"You always do."

Josephine was thankful Hannibal kept quiet. It was as if he willed her to be strong in the face of her aunt's bad attitude. This was a family fight, one that was long overdue. With Hannibal there, Josephine suddenly felt ready to take her aunt on.

Cordelia's eyes hit Josephine's face with the force of a blow. The girl was a rebel tonight. She was changing things. Cordelia did not like change. "The reverend—"

"Should mind his own business," Josephine finished.

Cordelia's neck corded with outrage. "Why you little . . . you little . . . strumpet."

A stunned Hannibal broke his uneasy silence. His voice was cordial, edged with ice. "Do you visit Josephine often?"

Cordelia had always been a big woman. Beneath Hannibal's regard, she felt frail and inconsequential. She did not want to feel frail. She did not want to feel as if she did not matter.

Hate turned her voice harsh. "You sure are bold asking me all sorts of questions like you've got a right and all." She humphed. She patted her pocketbook. "Handyman my foot."

The intrusion and the family fight were absolutely unreal to Hannibal. He glared back at Cordelia without a blink. He refused to be bullied. "If my being here isn't a problem for Josephine, why should it be a problem for you?"

Cordelia pretended she could not hear the question. "Josephine?" she said. "You need to be calling her Miss Brennon."

He rallied to Josephine's defense, even as he wondered what was wrong between the blood relatives. "If she doesn't have a problem, I don't have a problem."

Cordelia smacked her pocketbook against the table instead of smacking it against Hannibal the way she clearly wanted to do. "Um hum," she muttered between stiff lips. "We'll see what the reverend has to say about all this."

Slowly, deliberately, Hannibal stood from the

heirloom dining table. He did not like Cordelia's implied threat. She was in the wrong, not Josephine. He glanced at the woman who hired him. Maybe she literally was all alone, a thought which caused the flutter of his heart again.

Decisive, he removed the last piece of blue crockery from Josephine's hands, and was careful to touch her. His touch was one of compassion. As sure as the moon was full that night, he knew he was needed here.

He turned to Cordelia, the decision to stand up for Josephine on his mind, mischief in his eyes. He loved a good fight. "I can't wait to meet him."

SEVEN

The Brennon Farmhouse
Monday

Hannibal was dreaming. In the dream, Josephine knocked on his cottage door. From neck to ankle she wore shades of brown: a tan sweater, a walnut colored skirt, and dark chocolate boots. She fiddled with the red band confining her hair, as if nervous about how well he would receive her.

Smiling in welcome, Hannibal opened the door, all his attention focused on Josephine. "Good morning."

She returned his smile. "After the way my aunt caused a scene last night, I figured I'd better find out if you still want to work for me."

"I do." He stepped away from the partially open front door. "Come on in."

"I don't want to trouble you."

He closed the door. "You're no trouble."

In smooth strides, his palm at the small of her back, Hannibal ushered her deeper into his new home, a place that was quiet and stark in its simplicity.

"Your timing is perfect," he complimented. "I was just about to have cinnamon rolls and tea."

"Tea?"

He motioned to the hot plate he had used to warm a kettle of water. "Yep. Tea."

They moved to a small round table with two hard chairs. At the table, he laid out a Dixie paper plate topped with ready-made pastry. He sat two Styrofoam cups of freshly brewed orange spice tea beside the plate. The scene was as intimate and friendly as it was unplanned.

Inside the dream, Hannibal had the idea he might savor Josephine just as thoroughly as he savored the meal; only instead of savoring her in a chair at the table, he wanted to make love to her in the big bed which dominated the cottage.

The dream ended with Hannibal caught in a tangle of white cotton sheets. In his semi-awake state, he registered the fact that he was fully aroused and craving a woman he could never ask to share his bed.

Josephine was his employer, a woman who had hired him to make repairs to her property, period. She had given him no indication she wanted more than a business relationship.

Feeling melancholy after the dream, a dream so vivid he could almost believe it really happened, Hannibal stalked naked from the bed. At the window, he scanned the view outside.

It was 6:00 in the morning. The wind no longer howled. The ground, still damp with dew, was scattered with a plastic shopping bag, a sheet of newspaper, and the plastic rings from a six-pack of cans.

The first thing Hannibal planned to do after he dressed was to get rid of the trash the wind had blown onto the property during the night. As long as he was around, he wanted Josephine to have no greater worry than what she planned to feed the homeless.

And what about him? The dream forced Hannibal to consider the idea he wished for more than winter comfort. He desired Josephine, the only woman to make him dream in color.

His recent dream on his mind, Hannibal knocked on Josephine's kitchen door at eight-thirty in the morning. She opened her kitchen door with a smile so fine, he felt like a child at Christmas. "I stopped by to see if you need anything while I'm in town."

"No," she replied, then she stepped to the side so that he could enter her favorite place in a house she shared with no one. "Thanks anyway."

He remained right where he stood. There was a deeper truth to his standing there and he was man enough to say it. "I really just wanted to see you again."

Her left brow lifted in cool disregard. "Why?"

His early morning had been riddled with erotic dreams of Josephine, but he declined to tell her this disturbing bit of news. Instead he said, "I noticed you don't have a car. I haven't seen a bike. I was being polite."

"We went over everything last night about what you'd be doing today." She looked him over as if he had beans for brains. "Today, you're going to the hardware store for the odds and ends you need to do repairs around the property. I don't need a car, you do."

Hannibal's temper flashed. She was arrogant, not in an offensive or overbearing way like Cordelia Brennon, but arrogant in a disdainful way, as if she somehow held him in contempt. The way she looked him over, he had the feeling it was on the tip of her tongue to ask how dare he imply she could not take care of her personal needs without his help.

She was arrogant all right, but he had seen her in distress. Less than twelve hours before, he had witnessed a family fight that was so far from normal, he felt it placed him and Josephine slightly beyond the point of casual acquaintances. He was not about to let her throw his knowledge of that fight—and himself—under some rug.

She treated him far too casually. She was being way too snooty. She was lucky he kept himself from doing the one thing he really wanted to do: kiss that snooty look right off her haughty little face. He opted for the diplomatic approach instead. "I wanted to be sure you're okay."

"Why wouldn't I be?"

"When I was walking over the grounds this morning to make a list of things I want to buy at the building supply place in town, I saw your aunt's car. She was here at seven-thirty. After what happened last night, I wondered if something was wrong because she was here so early."

Josephine shrugged. "She was picking up cookies for a day-care center run by the Good Faith Baptist Church."

"Your aunt looked upset when she got into her car to leave."

"She often is upset."

Hannibal itched to shake Josephine, but accepted the truth instead. She was his employer and whatever she did short of breaking the law, was none of his business. He said, "When it gets down to it, it really shouldn't matter what I think is going wrong with you two. It's obvious there's bad blood between you guys."

She laughed, the sound low and throaty and derisive. "When you live in a small town like this one, everything is your business."

He said nothing, but his eyes were on fire.

"Come in and get comfortable," she said, her invitation breaking the dark silence between them. "I was making those cookies, so

I haven't had breakfast yet and Cordelia didn't want anything. Have a seat. I'll set the table."

"That's not necessary."

"Few things ever are."

She turned her slender back to him. By turning her back, she left it entirely up to him to sit down at the breakfast table or go on about his business of buying supplies to repair the property. Not even Mac Bishop was that confident or cold-blooded.

Hannibal's fists clenched in frustration. Josephine had to be the queen of one-liners. Beautiful, cryptic, alone, and poised, she was nothing he had encountered before in a woman. His first impression was that of a needy woman. His current impression was that she needed no one.

Hannibal eyed her in the same way he would eyeball a nearly impenetrable fortress: in precise detail. Dressed in brown, her only spot of color was her apron, which was printed with yellow cabbage roses, a flower he would always associate with Josephine. She too was a flower in winter, a thing of classic grace in an unusual setting.

Josephine had opened the kitchen door to him with a smile that gave him butterflies, then had walked away as if she could take him or leave him. Her armor was tough all right. Yet, something older than time let him know that she needed him. The knowledge came from the bone and went straight to his heart.

She was tough, but in him, she had met her match.

Hannibal threw down the proverbial gauntlet. His broad shoulders set, he entered her clean, scented kitchen, his stance that of a man who refused to be treated as if he had no more effect on his surroundings than the most gentle of breezes.

Breezes, he knew, could be deceiving. A breeze could run from light as a breath to moderate as a gust and from there to heavy as a gale. Like the wind, Hannibal would not be ignored.

The door to Josephine's kitchen door closed behind him with a decisive snap. Carefully, he removed his black Stetson, which he placed on a wood peg beside the door; still Josephine remained at the stove, either oblivious to the world or the best actress who ever lived.

He was incensed.

"Josephine."

He breathed the word, but she heard it.

Although she never stopped stirring the steaming silver pot on the stove, she did take time to answer. "Yes?"

"Never turn your back to me again."

Josephine stopped stirring the pot, her attention absolute. She was so accustomed to being ignored, it shocked her to discover she had come full circle by being rude herself. With a hint of the chagrin she felt at snubbing him, she said, "Coffee is ready."

He relaxed his stance. Removing his sheep-skin coat, he revealed a wide chest covered in red-checkered flannel over jeans so tight that Josephine saw the four corners of the wallet he kept in his butt pocket.

The scent of bread wafted from the lower deck of the stainless steel oven. Josephine's kitchen smelled snug and warm, the way his grandmother's kitchen had smelled to Hannibal. He had grown up with his parents and siblings, but it was his grandmother who had done most of the cooking.

"It smells great in here."

Josephine pointed at one of the chairs at the table in the nook where dishes were quickly set for them both. On the center of the table rested a cut crystal vase filled with small vines of English ivy.

"Coffee is all I need," he said. "I don't want you going to any trouble."

"Come on," she tempted him, "there's plenty of food."

The food she served was simple: creamy grits and smoked ham with strong black coffee. His eyes closed, Hannibal inhaled the steam rising from the heavy ceramic mug in his hand, then groaned his pleasure at the delicious scent.

When he opened his eyes, he found her staring at him with a hostess's appreciation. Dressed in brown, her hair pulled back with a rubber band, her basic grace and hospitality humbled him. He was a hired hand, but she treated him as her equal.

To lighten his mood, he said, "This is exactly what I needed to get myself going this morning." He had been reluctant to leave the property without making sure she was all right. Cordelia Brennon had set him on guard.

In response to his compliment, Josephine heaped his plate with more food. She served the elderly and the homeless, but this was her first chance to serve a man who made her skin tingle with physical awareness. She tried to hang on to the moment. "Take your time."

Hannibal ate enough grits and ham to stick to his stomach until dinner. "You're a good woman, Josephine."

"Thank you."

She was one of the kindest women he had met since leaving Half Dead. It was hard for him to think of a reason for anyone to start an argument with her the way Cordelia Brennon had done. Thinking about the fight that had broken up their quiet dinner pissed Hannibal off all over again. "Why do you put up with your aunt being rude to you?"

"It's no big deal."

"You can't downplay what happened last night," he argued, concern for her evident in his eyes. "I was there and I keep thinking about her threat to send the reverend, whoever he is."

"Aunt Cordelia always carries on like that when she isn't happy about something."

"Why is she unhappy?"

Josephine shrugged, then collected the dishes from the table she had set for two. "It doesn't matter."

He took his cue from the back she turned to him and rose from a table big enough to feed eight with room to spare. Once again, he had been dismissed, but this time, Hannibal refused to be ignored. "Josephine." His voice was black velvet, heavy and dark.

She met his gaze and was startled to find him so riled up. There was nothing she had done to him to cause such a dramatic shift in his attitude—was there?

"What is it, Hannibal?"

"This."

None too gently, he took her by the shoulders. Pressing her against his chest, Hannibal kissed Josephine until she had no idea if she was coming or going.

She savored the sensations; not even lightning, with all its electric energy, had the power to break the scintillating, breath-stealing moment she experienced in Hannibal's arms. She moaned, purred, forgot where she was completely.

In Hannibal's arms, Josephine's emotions soared a long way from Destiny, but this was not the case for Hannibal. Hannibal knew exactly where he was, exactly what he was doing.

With both hands, he gripped Josephine's butt. He squeezed the round goodness of it, then lifted her until her long brown legs wrapped around him.

A brief moment of clarity interrupted Josephine's surprise moment of surrender. She recognized that she had her legs wrapped around the waist of a man who was still new in town, but Lord Almighty, she felt good to do what she was doing.

There was a man in her kitchen, a man strong and black, a man that was hot like coffee. The only thing she could say was, "I . . . I—"

"—will be kissed like that every time you turn your back on me."

The black velvet of Hannibal's voice both soothed and captivated Josephine, and the unique sound of his voice drew her to him in the manner of kindred spirits.

The drifter was big enough to hurt her, bold enough to take her, but something in his old man's eyes spoke of honor and a natural-born grace. No, Josephine did not fear him, though she knew she should.

She should fear him because he was a stranger, because he made her lose every shred of her common sense. It was propriety that put an end to her brief bout of insanity. A prim expression on her face, Josephine unhooked her legs from his waist; she was lonely, not crazy.

Embarrassed, she ran a hand over the lowest part of her stomach, its center inundated with phantom butterflies. "Who are you?" she whispered before her breath caught in suspense; he had to be the most provocative man she had ever met.

The look his eyes threw down her body said Hannibal was anything she wanted him to be. His mouth said, "I'm the man who's gonna . . . fix your fence."

Satisfied he had shocked the flip out of her with his surprise kisses, Hannibal snatched his hat off the wood peg by the kitchen door. He squashed the hat down on his head, and swaggered from the room as if he could care less about what happened next. It was a magnificent act.

He cared more than he wanted to care about Josephine, more than he believed possible to care for a woman after being acquainted with her for barely a day. But then, Josephine was no ordinary woman, and her home was no ordinary home. Her home was its own brand of paradise.

In Josephine's paradise, Hannibal could almost believe that any dream was possible. All night long and into the dawn, he had dreamed about making love to Josephine. Those dreams had been drenched in color. Those dreams felt real, even in the broad light of day.

If Josephine thought it was arrogance that kept him from glancing back at her when he left the kitchen, she was wrong. He chose not to look back at her because he barely had the strength to keep his hands to himself.

He wanted to kiss her again and again, but common sense prevailed. He needed a job. She needed her fence fixed, a job he had placed on the top of his to-do list for the day.

Josephine watched him leave and was positive that arrogance kept him from looking back at her. As she watched him leave, she was torn between slapping his face for his arrogance and screaming for more of the same treatment.

If she could do both and get away with it, she would do it. Ever so slowly, Josephine slid the tip of her tongue between the soft crease of her lips.

Mmm, she thought. *Mmm.* The soft crease between her lips tasted of butter and cream, of smoked ham and spice—of Hannibal Ray on a Monday morning.

With trembling hands, Josephine righted her garments. She smoothed shaking fingers over her shining hair, her mind thankful the red rubber band holding her hair together was still in place. It was her lips that were not quite right. Her lips throbbed from Hannibal's expert kisses.

She touched a finger to her throbbing lips and felt shame. She had wrapped her legs around his waist. She had been so boneless, so utterly mindless that if he had released his arms from around her, she would have fallen straight to the floor. How could she face him again? What must he think of her?

Hannibal thought plenty, even though he tried not to think about Josephine at all. Whenever he thought about what happened in her kitchen, he had to adjust his crotch.

The ten-minute drive to the local hardware and building supply store was scenic. The bare branches of oak, maple, elm, willow, and sycamore trees gave him an unlimited view of three-story turn-of-the-century wood homes.

The mansions he saw were majestic. One home used an entire block as its foundation. Painted pure white, the home had a governor's mansion feel to it, yet in the front yard was a child's red wagon, discarded in-line skates, and a dog that entertained himself by barking at passing cars.

Two homes east of this mansion was a slim, yellow two-story as quaint as a little girl's Victorian-style doll house, complete with pastel gingerbread trim and decorative white picket fence. The fence reminded Hannibal of Josephine.

He had thought about her all through the night with a sense of pleasure combined with the surprising urge to look after her. The urge to protect her was as involuntary and natural a feeling to him as rain was as involuntary and natural to the earth it fed.

Never before had he felt such a primal need to protect a woman for the sake of his own satisfaction. However, it was his relationship with Rosalie that served as the stick Hannibal used to measure his intense attraction to Josephine.

Both women lived in small environments, but in comparison, it was Josephine who intrigued Hannibal the most. She intrigued him the same way a locked-room mystery intrigued him.

In a locked-room mystery, there was a closed environment. The closed environment in the mystery of Josephine was the Brennon farmhouse. Inside the century-old farmhouse lived a secretive young woman who kept herself hidden from the public eye—the question was *why?* Why did Josephine hide?

The obvious reason for her to hide was the scar on her face, but was that the only reason? Surely, Hannibal thought, in a town as small as Destiny, its residents would know about the scar on Josephine's face.

If the town residents knew about the scar, then the scar was not a secret. If the scar was not a secret, then why did Josephine hide away in a house far too big for one person to live in alone without getting lonely? The mystery of what made Josephine tick ran around and around Hannibal's mind. Because of this puzzle, he felt restless.

He turned his restless mind to Josephine's home, a building that was quietly running down, which was why he had cause to be in Josephine's life at all. He had stopped in Destiny because he was hungry and needed a job. He stayed in Destiny because he had found a job at the Brennon farmhouse, an aging place that was built for a family.

Based on her interaction with Cordelia Brennon, Hannibal reasoned that Josephine had no supportive family, a thought that appalled him. He had been raised to believe that members of a family respected one another, even when there was disagreement among the ranks.

For her to live alone, scarred and probably lonely, in a house that was beautiful but gradually falling apart, reinforced Hannibal's desire to look after Josephine.

The quiet drama of her self-contained lifestyle inspired him to feel compassion, a bittersweet sorrow that stirred within him unusually tender feelings, tender feelings that were sticky with questions.

The answer to the question *why* Josephine lived the way she did would be, for Hannibal, the key to the locked-room mystery of her life; but once he had the key—the answer to why she was a recluse—would his attraction to her fade?

It was too soon to tell if his attraction was a fleeting thing and it was none of his business anyway, but the fact that Josephine's private life was none of his business did not stop Hannibal from speculating about her. Somehow, despite her closed style of living, this haunting, perhaps even neurotic young woman had been brutally scarred.

The mystery behind that scar would not let Hannibal rest and neither would the story behind the house she shared with no one. She treated her house like a shrine, a shrine so meticulously cared for that even in winter, her roses still bloomed and her grass was still green.

For a seemingly unskilled, naive, ultra-ordinary woman, Josephine inspired intense emotions in the people immediately outside her circle of one—from the enemy who branded her, to the kin who mistreated her, to the stranger who sought to protect her.

Hannibal knew his judgments were snap, as her judgments had been snap when she hired him, but after so much dreaming during the night, dreaming which his waking thoughts now analyzed, Hannibal understood how she could hire him with no overthinking or deep conversations.

He wondered if she had hired him to repair her house when perhaps it was herself in need of the most repair. What if the ad in the Sunday newspaper had been a cry from Josephine for help? If instinct prompted him to protect her, then instinct could have prompted her to reach out to him for protection, to hire him on the spot.

In Hannibal's experience, profound and life-altering decisions were often based on involuntary impulses. The decision to enter a burning building to save an elderly woman, to stop the brutal beating of a stranger, to walk on thin ice to save a drowning child, were all decisions commonly acted on by the impulse to react first and think about consequences later.

Right now, Hannibal was acting on impulse. He would deal with the consequences later.

His dreaming had not been wasted. The throwing down of the proverbial gauntlet in Josephine's kitchen had been the right thing to do—instinct told him so. Instinct, that involuntary impulse that opposed the science of reason, told him he was on the right track.

Nothing Hannibal felt about Josephine was reasonable or scientific. For the first time, he was winging it on a new frontier, the frontier of an unusual relationship with an unusual woman.

The compassion he felt for her, the urge to protect her, and the erotic way he craved her were all out-of-the ordinary experiences for him. They were outside the realm of his self-control.

Because these experiences were out of the

ordinary, he saw them as worthy of deep thought. Hannibal knew they were worthy of deep thought because he knew himself well. He knew he was the kind of man who played for keeps.

Josephine was too complex a woman for him to pick up for a few months and then put down for the rest of his life without some type of emotional consequence.

There had to be a strong reason he had tossed away the perfectly good relationship he once enjoyed with Rosalie Jones. Maybe, he mused, just maybe, Josephine was that reason.

How else could Rosalie, a woman Hannibal considered a hero, be cast in the shadow of his mind almost completely? He had known Josephine for one day—just one—and yet he understood what it was for her to be lonely, to be restless.

Maybe he understood because, after all, he was a rambling man. So once again, he considered the yellow farmhouse, its rural postcard perfection marred by the crack in the second-story window.

Despite the little he knew about Josephine, there was no way Hannibal could leave town without answers to his many questions. He had to know if justice had been served in defense of the scar on her face.

To know if justice had been served in honor of Josephine, he had to first find out the truth about why her face was so badly scarred. To get at the truth, he had to dig at her secrets.

To gain access to her secrets, he had to make Josephine understand that once he was a friend, he was a friend for life; she could trust him. The thought of winning her trust made him smile.

From this point on, he would make Josephine's happiness his personal business. She deserved to know that she mattered. Right or wrong, illogical or not, she did matter to him, and somehow, the feeling felt right.

EIGHT

The Brennon Farmhouse
The Same Day
1:30 PM

Reverend Franklin arrived at Josephine's home with fire and brimstone. Sister Shirley Louise was fire. Sister Bea was brimstone. The three walked into the house, their eyes silently cataloging what was the same and what was different about their reception. Nothing was different.

As usual, Josephine graciously allowed them into her home. Once they were seated in the living room, she set the coffee table with refreshments. Since cooking and baking were her business as well as her hobby, Josephine rarely was without food to share.

Josephine's only surprise was that the trio had not come at dawn, perhaps hoping for gossip, like finding a strange man in the scarred woman's bed. The trio looked disappointed to find her in the house by herself.

The Christian sisters sat on the sofa, the reverend and Josephine in matching chairs facing them. On the small table between the uncomfortable group were plates of cookies, buttermilk pie, and almond butter toffee Josephine had made from scratch. She loved almond toffee, a secret reinforcement for the battle presented by her guests.

The sisters started their interrogation of their hostess with the crack in the upstairs window. "How come that window ain't fixed yet, Josephine?"

The woman of the house paused before giving her answer to a question that drew a hard line between herself and the others. The line confirmed that her guests were on their own twisted terms. It was social business as usual. Because of those terms, the three visitors were able to draw strength from each other.

Josephine drew strength from the living room. It was her space to do with whatever she wanted. The colors were the same as those she wore every day of the week. They were brown, cream, faded yellow, with slivers of red. To her, they were restful colors.

She only flicked a brow at her guest's sharp tone. "The window will get fixed in time, Sister Shirley Louise."

"Snap to it girl, my tea is cold."

"I'll pour you another, Sister Bea." Josephine added one teaspoon of sugar to the sister's orange pekoe tea, which she served in cups of soft white Lennox china.

Sister Shirley Louise spoke with a mouth full of candy. The candy did little to sweeten her tongue. "How come that fence isn't up yet, Josephine?"

"Hannibal is out right now buying wood to fill the gaps, Sister Shirley Louise." Josephine imagined the ingredients in her almond candy: the butter, the sugar, the broken almonds. It was a meditation that soothed her during a situation that tested her nerves and skills in social grace.

"Well?" the sister prompted.

"A post broke and had to be replaced," Josephine said, thinking she was glad he was not there to be scrutinized.

After Aunt Cordelia, she did not want him to think that working with her was going to be too much trouble to bother with. Being a drifter, he was tied to no special place. By his own admission, no woman claimed his name. He did not have to stay.

"When's he coming back?" Sister Bea demanded.

They had almost come to Josephine's place for nothing. The consolation prize for their efforts was the excellent tea, the quality food, and the confirmation that Josephine did in fact have a man in residence on her property.

"He'll be back anytime now."

The reverend, content until now to stuff as

much food into his stomach as would comfortably fit, pushed his crumb-filled plate of what was left of his buttermilk pie to the side of the pine coffee table.

He thought of a man in Josephine's home, and that this man was probably the only new addition she had brought into her home in a very long time. It shocked the reverend to realize Josephine was sitting on a collector's dream of home furnishings and bric-a-brac.

The tables were solid pine and extremely well-crafted. The dishes in her curio were family heirlooms: Fostoria, Carnival, Blue Willow. It was all old but somehow the way she used them gave the impression of keepsakes that were only gently used.

Her gleaming wood floors were scattered with rugs to keep her feet from getting cold if she ever ran barefoot in her house during winter. Josephine in her bare feet was something the reverend had never seen.

When had he last seen Josephine smile? Had he ever? Too much introspection brought up too many bad memories and so the reverend switched his thoughts from the blandness of Josephine's life to the richness of Josephine's food.

He belched, satisfied with the warm feeling in his stomach. He was equally satisfied with the brash interrogation of Josephine by Sister Shirley Louise and Sister Bea. All he had needed to do was show up, then listen to the dirty work being done. It was his role to be objective.

"More pie?" Josephine asked the reverend, a fcather-thin man she felt she had known forever.

He rubbed his potbelly stomach with a hand covered in diamond rings, the one on his pinkie shaped like a cross. It was his favorite piece of jewelry. "I couldn't hold another bite."

Josephine's smile was the essence of all things good in the world, but her eyes, her eyes were banked with fire. She wanted to scream at them to leave her alone.

Because she did not attend church, the trio made it their business to minister to Josephine at her home. Always, they were uninvited. Josephine knew they really came out of a warped sense of duty and for the generous portions of food she served them.

Coming to Josephine's house was a break from their everyday lives. It was also something very few people got to do in Destiny; walk through the white picket fence, over the stone walk, up the wide wood stairs, past the gingerbread porch rail, and through the yellow-painted front door.

In truth, the trio felt honored; but today Josephine had no desire in her heart to humor them. By coming to her house because Cordelia Brennon had sicced the reverend on her, Josephine faced the fact that they were and had always been people who were destructive forces in her life.

She was restless, so very restless. She wished she had the courage of Hannibal, a man who did what he wanted to do whenever he felt like doing it. If she had his courage to speak her mind, she would tell her guests what she really thought about them.

Thinking of Hannibal, of his freedom from nosy do-gooders like Shirley Louise and Bea, inspired Josephine to act on her suppressed animosity. She said, demurely and softly spoken as ever, "More tea, sisters?"

"No."

"No."

"Then you won't mind me getting back to work. I have vegetables to chop for dinner."

The sisters gasped.

Josephine moved with all the finesse of a servant well skilled in the art of serving others with an economy of motion. There was very little clinking of dishes as she picked up her silver serving tray, another Brennon heirloom, and stacked the gleaming metal with dirty linen napkins, dirty Lennox china, and the remaining crumbs from the buttermilk pie.

The reverend watched the proceedings with all the shock of the Christian sisters, but he was much more adept at hiding his feelings. Something new was going on with Josephine. She was different, feisty, intriguing; but then, she had always been intriguing to him.

He understood how she ended up in Destiny. An orphan was often sent packing to live with relatives, near or distant, but why had she stayed? He never understood why. Looking at her now, he had an idea about why she stayed. It was so unexpected he was not sure what to think.

What if Josephine, quiet, humble, submissive Josephine, had stayed in Destiny to punish those who had been unkind? She did not have to hide in the house because of the scar on her face, because the scar could be removed by cosmetic surgery.

She had to know that the sight of her damaged flesh was a constant reminder that a very certain evil had been carried out in secret, a secret that had not yet been brought into the light of public scrutiny.

She could easily have pointed out her abuser and yet she was silent as the grave about the pain inflicted upon her in her youth. All she had ever had to do was point one finger and the town would have descended on her abuser like vultures to carrion.

The reverend tapped his palm against his spindle-thin knee. In his mind, he saw the cottage at the end of the kitchen walk, where the herbs from Josephine's garden flourished in the winter light. Josephine kept a man in that cottage.

Shirley Louise and Bea had come to turn a scrap of dirt on Josephine into big gossip. He had come to see the drifter.

The drifter.

Josephine's handyman was a stranger in a strange land, perhaps even the catalyst for Josephine's changed behavior. Thinking of the man he had yet to meet, the reverend slid his eyes over Josephine. "Still feeding the homeless, I gather." They all knew he was referring to Hannibal.

"You know I am."

"Sister Cordelia said you were all vinegar lately," the reverend noted. "The question is, why?"

"Or why not?" the scarred woman countered, her voice smooth as new silk thread.

"This isn't like you to be rude, Josephine," Sister Bea admonished, her tone that of a person in absolute shock.

Sister Shirley Louise backed her buddy up with a brief nod of her slick, bobbed wig. She was not so much stunned by Josephine's behavior as she was scandalized. Josephine was tame. Josephine was nobody. Who did she think she was, giving them the boot? She was lucky they bothered to visit her at all. She should feel blessed.

The younger woman touched her scarred cheek, and the sisters looked away. The reverend winced.

"Perhaps," Josephine softly said, not looking at any one person in particular, "that's the point."

NINE

The Same Day
1:30 PM

Hannibal worried about Josephine the entire time he selected the wood he needed to repair her broken fence. The men who helped him select posts, replacement boards, and entire sections of fence at the lumberyard had known right away he was new to Destiny.

His truck had Texas plates on it for one thing. For another, the men who labored beside him did not know his name. Destiny was too small a town to attract a stranger in search of lumber.

In an attempt to shake off his growing sense of doom over a woman he knew little about, Hannibal focused on his paid assignment. Systematically, he cruised the lumberyard and its adjacent hardware store, places he would be visiting often for supplies while working for Josephine.

But on the drive back from the lumberyard,

his thoughts returned to Cordelia Brennon. The idea that a grown woman, especially blood kin, would mistreat Josephine was not okay. As long as he was around, Hannibal vowed it would not happen again.

He spotted the late-model luxury car before he rounded the corner to Josephine's house. He pulled his truck to a stop behind the car. Sparkling silver with light gray leather seats, the late-model Lincoln Town Car looked as out of place and unwelcome as a weasel in a hen house. There was a nervous tension in Hannibal's body. He had the uncanny feeling that Cordelia Brennon's threat to send the reverend had not been an idle one.

He wished he knew why Josephine was hated so much. Did her scar embarrass her relatives? Had her abuser gone unpunished and as a result her family, Aunt Cordelia in particular, thought Josephine was somehow to blame?

With solemn deliberation, Hannibal considered his options. As a handyman, it was not his place to inquire about Josephine's guests. Maybe he should just unload the fence material and go on about the work he had been hired to do; but then, that was impossible. He was already hooked.

He decided to unload the fence supplies later. Crushing his black Stetson to his head, Hannibal left his truck. Stomping the red dirt from his creased leather boots, he took the wide steps to Josephine's lovely front door two steps at a time. He was in a hurry because he had the feeling it was finally time to meet the reverend.

Worry made Hannibal bold. He strode through Josephine's front door without stopping to knock first, but smiled as soon as he spotted her. His feet came to a stop within the circle of her private space and there, in a room filled with Josephine's enemies, he singled out the scent of her warm brown body. For an instant, it seemed to him that she smelled of heaven itself. She was more than all right; she was calm and glad to see him.

"Hello, Josephine." He gazed at her as if he wanted to say, *Don't be afraid.*

A witness to the surprised wonder on her face, Reverend Franklin stopped putting on the gray leather jacket, which fell to the knees of his gray dress slacks. "This is your handyman?" His voice ended on a note so high there was a squeak to it.

Hannibal extended his hand, which the reverend was slow to take. "That's right, sir," he confirmed, "I'm here to take care of whatever she needs." He was not the only one who could be cryptic.

The reverend's grip was soft, the gesture purely an automatic one as he sized up the younger man. Based on Cordelia Brennon's description, he half expected that Josephine had taken up with a loser straight off the streets of Destiny.

With this image in mind, the reverend anticipated a wiry hustler, a man with a neglected air about him, a scraggly beard, or tobacco-stained teeth. He expected a man with a conniving look in his eyes, a man out to take advantage of Josephine.

But when confronted with Hannibal, the reverend realized he should have been worried that the man had no past in Destiny. A man with no past was a man with no roots.

A man with no roots was a dangerous man, which is exactly how Hannibal looked to the reverend: tall, tough, and totally relaxed. Hannibal was big enough to take on another man his size or bigger and figure he could win. He was tough enough to tackle Cordelia Brennon, a woman the people of Destiny tried to keep on their good side.

The reverend shook hands with Hannibal but he did not like it. The younger man's skin felt so rough it scratched the soft palm of the sixty-plus elder of the Good Faith Baptist Church.

That brief, firm handshake confirmed to the reverend that Josephine's handyman was not a drug addict in search of work to support a habit. He was clean, well-spoken, and bold as the devil himself the way he walked into his employer's house without knocking.

Even Cordelia knocked on her niece's front door, a fact the reverend had given no thought to until now. Rude as she was to Josephine,

Cordelia Brennon was still on her guard, always, but for what?

After all these years, what was it Cordelia feared? Was she afraid that if she chose not to announce herself with a knock on Josephine's front door she might come into the house to find her niece dead by suicide, a death explained by the despair of living alone without real friends or any hope of feeling beautiful in a caring man's eyes?

Or did Cordelia knock on Josephine's front door as an act of selfish power at having made the young, scarred woman stop whatever she was doing not only to answer her front door, but to invite the enemy inside for another session of bad behavior?

The reverend curtailed his thoughts. None of those issues mattered right now. Right now there was a strange man in Josephine's house, a man who looked as if he might never leave her side.

The stranger's presence shifted the reverend's perspective of Josephine as an individual. This was the first time since she was a child that he had seen a smile in her eyes or heard pride in her voice over something other than the food she cooked for the lonely.

The reverend said with the hushed tone of a man speaking to the sick, "Have you lost your mind, Josephine?"

"Only if you have, Reverend," she quipped. Sister Shirley Louise pulled the pink handkerchief from the front pocket of her matching suit jacket. She fanned her face with the handkerchief, all the while muttering, "Lord, Lord, Lord, what's gotten into this child?"

"Amen," said Sister Bea. She buttoned her navy wool coat to the neck. She was halfway to the front door before she realized Reverend Franklin and Sister Shirley Louise were not to the left and right behind her. Still, she kept her hand on the crystal knob of the front door, a silent statement that she was ready to go.

Josephine heard the squeak in the reverend's voice. She relished the surprised sound of it. "Yes, sir," she said. There was pride in her own voice, pride low-keyed, but unmistakable.

She swept her gaze to the source of contention between her and her guests. The reverend had always been smug with her, self-righteous in his weekly endeavors to minister to her while he stuffed himself with her cakes, pies, cookies, and other things sweet.

He often asked her to stir his coffee with her finger because she was sweeter to him than any candy. She would give him another lump of sugar to sweeten his coffee and pretend she never heard him say he wanted a taste of her finger.

In all her years of knowing the reverend, Josephine wished time and time again that she had the nerve to shock him with the truth about her feelings for him. She could not stand his pretense of pity over the woman she had become during her stay in Destiny, a scarred woman afraid to leave home.

She despised the way he used religion to excuse the ugly in himself. Josephine believed in God. She had no faith in Reverend Franklin, a man she knew as one of the biggest hypocrites in the town; they shared in an uneasy truce, but no more.

These days, Josephine felt too restless to maintain the status quo. She was ready to live again, despite her fear. It was precisely because of her loneliness that she had placed the ad in the tiny, overpriced newspaper, which delivered to her door a man with the gift of salvation.

Hannibal knew none of her secrets, had no idea who the guests were in her home, but he had sensed trouble. He had come in from the cold to warm her with the fire of life.

His zest for living and for adventure inspired Josephine to stand up for herself. It was long past time she took control of the rest of her life. She did not want to be alone anymore. She did not want to be afraid.

She glanced at Hannibal and took courage from his relaxed pose. He was relaxed because he had no past with the reverend or the sisters. He had no reason to care what made the reverend or the sisters tick. He cared only about Josephine. She was the reason he barged through her front door as if he owned the place.

A compelling man to watch from any angle, Hannibal was tall, dark as good rum, and hardy as a buffalo soldier. His seen-everything-done-everything gaze bowled over Josephine's guests as if he saw straight through each one of them. He surveyed the silent room with the intensity of a predatory animal. He stared at them as if he had viewed every living threat in the world not once but twice.

His gaze was arrogant, yes, but there was an ageless grace about his personality that softened his male pride, a grace that won him a place in Josephine's troubled heart. Buffed, strong, virile, and totally rugged, he tipped the scales of justice in Josephine's favor when he grinned at her for all he was worth.

It had been a long time since he'd battled with his wits instead of his fists. The last time had been when he'd argued with Rosalie Jones about how the lilies should be planted in her water barrel.

Outnumbered three to one, Josephine needed a good friend, Hannibal figured. He turned off his handsome smile in order to concentrate on the reverend, the man he figured was the most powerful enemy of the trio that confronted Josephine on behalf of Cordelia Brennon.

Briefly, he wondered how a woman as tame as Josephine could have four people in her life who hated her so much they went out of their way to make her life miserable. The idea that four grown people could enter someone else's home with the sole purpose of harassment was shocking to him.

Hannibal was a fair man, the kind of man who stepped up when a woman was in distress. He had no intention of leaving her alone in a hostile room.

Josephine studied her handsome new friend with rapt admiration. She had never known a hero she could call her own. She took a step nearer to his side. There were two feet of space between them, but by standing in his private space, she too had crossed a line. By choosing to stand at Hannibal's side, she had become an outsider.

Outsiders were new people in Destiny. The simultaneous looks of shock on the faces of the reverend and his Christian sisters were a breath of fresh air for Josephine. She owed it all to Hannibal. He had not chosen to be simply a handyman. He had chosen to be her friend.

In the awkward silence of her living room, with its heirloom furniture, dirty serving dishes, and confounded guests, Josephine concentrated on his physical presence. His nearness caused her heart to feel . . . wonderful. Just as he had stood up for her to Aunt Cordelia, he quietly measured the worth of Josephine's guests.

Each one of them had so much nerve that the basic goodness in Hannibal Ray rebelled against the unfairness of it all. The anger within him joined forces with his basic goodness, altering his personal strength into a force strong enough for Josephine to tap into and not feel alone.

Hannibal gave no thought to being a savior. He knew for a fact he was not a saint, but he was human and caring and sincere in his intentions toward Josephine.

Unlike her guests, spiritual icons within Destiny, he would never harm her. No man would harm her as long as he had the power to do anything about it, which he did. His decision to back Josephine red-flagged his integrity. In Hannibal, integrity was a virtue, an essential piece of his personal power.

His energy renewed Josephine. She welcomed the beginnings of her newfound strength. How often did a man meet a woman branded with the letter X? Probably never.

How many men could witness such a mark and not ask the awful reason behind it? Few. However, he asked nothing about her face. Instead of putting her on the spot, he made her feel so . . . worthy. He made her feel so . . . fine. With slender fingers, hesitant in their movements, Josephine touched the red rubber band that imprisoned her hair, and wished she could let it go.

The reverend noticed the gesture. He was

comforted by this familiar habit. Josephine played with her hair when she was uneasy. Being uneasy around people was natural for her. It was expected.

The reverend flicked fake dust off the expensive leather of his fancy jacket. "We're leaving."

Josephine and Hannibal spoke together. "Good."

The sisters gasped.

The reverend's mouth fell open.

Their consternation was food to Josephine's starved and wrinkled soul. She did something that surprised everyone, including herself. She laughed.

Hannibal threw open the front door. As the sisters stomped out, he could not resist saying, "Next time ladies, leave your brooms at home."

Sister Shirley Louise said, "We'll pray for you, young man."

"Yes," her cohort agreed. "We'll pray."

Hannibal used one of Josephine's polite give-nothing-away one-liners. "Thank you."

The reverend said nothing. He just left.

Hannibal watched the Lincoln edge from the curb before turning to face the object of his growing obsession. She beamed at him. She had a lovely smile. "Josephine?"

"Yes?"

"Let's pack up and go." He saw the look in her eyes. They were bright, hungry, eager eyes.

"Where?"

He opened his long arms wide, his spirit as carefree as the wind. "Canada. Vermont. Anywhere."

Her heart pounded against her breast. He offered her a choice, to stay miserable or to join him in an adventure of their own making. She wanted to go with him. The urge was so powerful her skin tingled with the effort to keep still. Did she dare grab life with both hands? "No."

Disappointment pierced his small bubble of joy. As far as he could tell, there was nothing to tie her to Destiny. She could get into his truck right now and nobody would track her down. "Why?"

She could face him no more, this honest, clean-living man who made her want to shake her head until her hair fell down. "I can't run from the past. It's why I stay. It's who I am."

"What you're saying doesn't make sense." Anger burned a path through his bones. He hated to see a perfectly healthy woman throw her life away. His family had always been good to him, good for him. It was because of his strong beginnings in life that he knew it was fruitless to look backward, only forward. "Nobody can be the past."

Josephine had years of experience with pissed-off people. She made no effort to appease him any more than she bothered to appease the reverend or the sisters. This was her house, her life. "I can."

She stacked dishes as if she were alone in the living room. He bet she would keep stacking those dishes even if he left her house for good, a tempting thought.

He had no real wish to involve himself in a drama centered around a confused young woman too scared to grab life with both hands. Still, he had to try. He really did want to understand. "You've got to break this down for me, Josephine. Help me understand."

Despite everything, she wanted his approval, wanted him to keep on being her hero. She wanted him to open those big arms of his and take her back inside them, to wrap her up in a brand-new kind of love. She had been desperate for love for so long she had no idea how to act now that it was staring her in the face. Pride held her in check. "I didn't ask for your help."

It was all he could do not to shake her. Did she not know she deserved more than a lifetime of near-total solitude? "Yes, you did ask for help," he said, referring to the ad in the newspaper.

"I didn't ask you to stay."

"True."

"So go." The words were out before she could stop them.

He placed his hands on her shoulders. They were tense. He had no explanation for how or why, but he understood this woman. Beneath her thorns were soft, succulent feelings and a fragile heart. To keep from getting herself hurt, she was pushing him away. The knowledge cemented his fate. "Not without you."

Oh, how he made her want things she had never had: a committed relationship, children, a rich and full life. "And you say I don't make any sense. You don't know me from a hole in the wall, but you expect me to run off into the blue yonder because you say so. I've got a house to run. I've got people to feed."

He wanted to argue that her aunt could run the house. The churches could feed the homeless and the elderly. She could go anyplace she wanted to go if she could scrounge up the nerve to do it. He chose to highlight the obvious. "You have no life."

She thought of the fresh air he brought into her slice of paradise. "Oh yes I do, handyman. Yes, I do."

He clenched his fists, opened them, clenched them. "I don't like riddles, Josephine."

"So go fix the fence."

She was cayenne pepper in a plain brown wrapper. Brown skirt, brown shirt, brown shoes, and long beautiful hair trapped in a red rubber band. He broke that red band before she had time to blink, stole a kiss before she could protest, and was halfway to the door when she grabbed his arm. "Wait!"

He looked down into eyes that made him feel larger than life. Common sense told him to get a hundred miles away from Josephine Brennon, but common sense had no control right now, those allspice-colored eyes of hers did. "Yeah?"

She could think of nothing to say. She just wanted him to stay, wanted him to believe she was more than a gutless wonder. "This." She grabbed his face between her hands, pulled him toward her, and kissed him—hard.

He wrapped her in his arms, her hair trapped against his chest. "Josephine."

She relished the way he said her name. Deeply. Darkly. Possessively. She shivered, desire running thick and heady as sweet vintage wine; but then he touched her scar with his lips. The touching of her scar killed her desire instantly.

She shoved him away. "Don't!"

"Josephine."

Her hand covered the scar. Tears filled her eyes, tears that could not conceal the fact that she believed she was ugly. Josephine ran from the living room into the kitchen, her sanctuary.

He wanted to follow, to take her in his arms again, but he knew solitude had its time, and the time was now. Hannibal returned to his truck, determined to fix Josephine's fence, determined to make room for himself in Josephine's paradise.

TEN

The air in the master bedroom smelled of sex and talcum powder. Cordelia Brennon stared at the reverend with stormy eyes that boded trouble for him. He had been tiptoeing around the subject of Josephine from the moment they came together that afternoon.

Unwilling to do battle, he sat silently beside her at the foot of the bed. The sheets on the bed were damp with sweat. The chenille bedspread, charcoal gray in color, was twisted so that half of it lay on the bed while the other half lay on the floor, right next to the reverend's leather bedroom slippers.

The slippers matched the bedspread, which matched the paint on the walls. The only significant color in the room was burgundy. Cordelia hated the color burgundy. She hated the reverend's bedroom, period.

They never went anywhere, not even to another town, for fear someone either of them knew might catch them and tell the rest of the busybodies in town. Right now, he was worse than a busybody because he had her undivided attention. She had no desire to hear what he had to say about Josephine or her hired hand.

She wanted to hear that he was still on her side of the line she had drawn between herself and her niece. The silence in the room was heavy. The silence did not bother Cordelia. She used the absence of words in the room to ground herself.

With sharp, agitated movements, she pulled on her navy blue lace girdle. It was so tight it made her thighs itch from lack of circulation. She had no wish to spend her last few minutes with the reverend talking about Josephine, but she had no one else she could trust. "What are you gonna do about that little hussy?" she demanded.

Thinking of Josephine, the reverend's thin shoulders sagged just a little. He could be controlled with sex, but hatred had never motivated him to take action against another human being the way it did Cordelia. Her hatred for Josephine was blind.

Over the years, Cordelia's obsession with Josephine had been the bond that kept him and Cordelia together year after year. Sex eased the tension of their less-than-scrupulous arrangement. The reverend doubted Hannibal

Ray would give up his honor for so small a favor.

Hannibal was different. He struck the reverend as the kind of guy who would not let sex make him do wrong. The stranger had been protective of Josephine. A man who protected a woman he barely knew against people she knew well was not the kind of guy who built his life around secrets.

In contrast, the reverend brooded, he was in the secret-keeping business. Through his work, he heard many details about private lives that would hurt if the truth came to light.

Hannibal carried himself like a man with nothing to hide. Thinking of Hannibal Ray, a younger man, a man with no past in Destiny, the reverend sensed it was time to step down from his role in Josephine's life.

He had never enjoyed his role anyway, that of being mean for mean's sake. "Why don't you leave that girl alone, Cordelia?" It made perfect sense after all these years.

"I can't," she argued, her face to the wall. "You know full well that girl is just like Marvella." She said the last as if she was ashamed to speak the words.

With an air of distraction, the reverend walked over to a mahogany chifforobe, opened a drawer, and removed his favorite navy suspenders. Collecting suspenders was his hobby.

He had suspenders that were a hundred years old, but the navy pair was new, custom made. The pair he chose matched the girdle on Cordelia Brennon's thick thighs. It was an unconscious selection, but one he would understand if he thought about it.

He liked thick thighs, Cordelia's in particular, and he often wondered why she worried so much about the fit of her dress when it was her eyes that drove people away, not her body.

He thoroughly enjoyed the hills, curves, and valleys of her plus-sized body, which was half the reason his bedroom smelled like sex most Wednesday afternoons.

He liked having sex with Cordelia because she let him be human. She let him relax completely. She let him be himself because she knew for a fact that he was flawed and frail, not the demigod many of his church flock considered him to be.

Cordelia wanted nothing to do with a demigod in her bed. She wanted a red-blooded man and in return for sexual service, she demanded only silence. Today was different. Like Josephine, the reverend was restless. "Marvella is dead, Cordelia. Josephine don't have nobody but you and you treat her like garbage."

Cordelia yanked the sheets into place on the bed. It appeared she and the reverend were going to fight anyway. She had no desire to fight with her lover so soon after making love. "Humph. As well she should be—"

"Cordelia!"

The chenille bedspread snapped in the air.

"The girl is just like Marvella. Josephine is chasing after a worthless drifter, just like my sister did when she went chasing some worthless piano player—"

"Cordelia!"

Snap. Snap. "—roaming from one run-down hole-in-the-wall town to another until she screwed her life up completely."

"Now, Cordelia," the reverend said in a warning tone, "you know full well it ain't none of Josephine's fault she was born out of wedlock."

Cordelia grabbed the burgundy toss pillows from the floor and threw them at her lover, who calmly replaced them at the head of the bed. Now that the bed was made, another uneasy silence held center stage.

Cordelia was absolute in her self-righteousness, her backbone straight as ever. "Bad things come from bad people."

The reverend snapped fourteen-karat gold cuff links into place at his skinny yellow wrists. "Weren't you the one who wanted the piano player?" He remembered the past quite plainly, but he chose to goad his top-secret lover for his own twisted pleasure.

Cordelia stopped reapplying her makeup in the oval antique mirror. She spun around so fast a line of red lipstick smeared her bug-eyed face. "What?"

Spite drove the reverend to goad her further. "And didn't the piano player want your sister, Marvella, instead of you?" Marvella was dead and gone, but Cordelia held on to her spite with all the blind tenacity of the Hatfields and the McCoys.

She went after her black patent leather pocketbook as if her life depended on getting out of the reverend's house in no time flat. "Hold on a cotton-pickin' minute!"

It was rare to get Cordelia in a huff, which was the reason the reverend enjoyed his spiteful game. "No! You hold on a minute, Cordelia Brennon. Don't you forget I know every little thing about you."

Cordelia stopped at the door, her hand on its brass handle, her back straighter than a split stick of firewood. "I know every little thing about you, too."

The reverend grabbed Cordelia's arm. Not at all gentle, he forced her to face him. Cold, gray eyes met angry black ones in a silent battle that had raged since the coming of Josephine. "Marvella was your sister. She deserves your respect."

"She stole Stud Bishop from me."

"The way I see it, Stud Bishop didn't want to be had."

"He—"

"Got what he wanted from you and Marvella. That worthless son of a gun kept on fooling around until he destroyed a relationship between two sisters. That ain't Josephine's fault."

Cordelia tried to shake her arm loose from the reverend's grip, but he held fast, determined to have his say. "Stud abandoned Marvella when she needed him most. He didn't give a hoot about Josephine. The man wasn't worth all the trouble he caused."

Again Cordelia tried to shake her arm loose. Again the reverend staked his claim on her arm. The flesh trapped between his fingers was no longer as firm as when they first began their midday trysts in his cast-iron bed nearly twenty years before. "Some men can't be held, Cordelia."

She tossed her freshly powdered nose in the air. She was haughty, strong, mad at the world because she had not been born beautiful, as Marvella had been beautiful.

When she tried to avert her gaze, the reverend grabbed her chin. His voice was as quiet as their secret sins. "You've got to accept the natural fact that some men were born to be free."

"Is that what you want," she demanded, tears in her angry eyes, "to be free?"

"Ain't no way I can be free. Not with you coming in and out of my house like it's yours."

The skin beneath Cordelia's right eye twitched with a new wave of anxiety. "Nobody suspects—"

He flatly refused to hear whatever she had to say on the subject. "Do you honestly believe that our Wednesday romps are a secret?"

"We discuss the homeless and the menu and the—"

Disgusted, he released her arm. "Don't insult me or yourself. I've got an office and a secretary at the church. You don't need to come to the house, especially not alone."

"But it's so early in the day. Nobody would think of such a thing."

"Nobody but you. Secrets ain't just made in the dark. You think that because we're meeting out in the open people think we're being honest, too. Nobody in town is that stupid."

Her black eyes had a sheen of moisture to them. He was right, but she just had no wish to hear it, not now, not when she felt so vulnerable and alone. "But—"

"No buts, Cordelia," the reverend said in disgust.

He was not moved by a woman's tears, perhaps because he saw so many of them in his line of work. Women cried from pleasure as easily as they cried from anger or pain. He was oblivious to all three, which was the reason he scarcely registered the water in Cordelia's desperate eyes. He said, "One thing you've never been is naive."

"Marry me."

He cut her a you've-got-to-be-kidding glare. His hands fisted at his sides, opened, then fisted again as if he wanted to take her by the shoulders and shake her. "What?"

"Marry me."

"I heard you the first time, Cordelia. I just can't believe you've got the nerve to be asking me to marry you after all this time."

"Well?" she prompted. If ever a man understood her, he was the man. She had too many secrets to keep and so did he. They were made for each other, only she could not get him to commit beyond their Wednesday afternoon sex routine.

"I know too much about you to want to marry you." He sounded every bit as disillusioned as he felt. Why did she have to mess things up by adding one more complication to an already messed-up relationship. It was too late to go public now.

"Well, just hurt my feelings, why don't you." Tough as Cordelia was on the outside, only this man had the power to lay her feelings low. She sniffed, the sound half genuine, half act. She never really expected him to say he would marry her.

The reverend felt the weight of every problem he had ever heard during his ten-year preaching stint at Good Faith Baptist Church. Most of all, he felt the weight of his own complex burdens. Wednesday-afternoon sex with Cordelia was both pleasure and pain.

The physical pleasure released his tensions right up until it was time to get dressed, like now. It was afterward that he would feel the pain of his own betrayals.

Cordelia reminded the reverend that despite

his position within Destiny's spiritual community, he would have hell to pay on Judgment Day. "You don't have any feelings, Cordelia."

She looked at him as if he were losing his mind faster than he could put on his shoes. "What is wrong with you today?"

"Everything."

"Humph," she grumbled. "You were fine when you were smacking my butt and hollering giddy-up a minute ago."

"Forget it."

She cocked her head to the side, her eyes doing a slow move over his face, his posture. The man looked fed up with the world and himself, too. "Truth be told, you were fine up until you went to see Josephine with Shirley Louise and Bea."

Temper put a hard edge to his voice. "I'm serious, Cordelia. Leave it alone."

In all their Wednesday afternoons together in his house—years of them—the reverend had never verbally told her to get out of his house. He always ended their sessions together by opening his bedroom door, then guiding her out with his hand at the small of her back.

It was a courtly ritual she welcomed and waited for because she knew that in some small way she had pleased him. Pleasing him meant they would have another Wednesday together. Today was different. She thought she knew why. "You're afraid of the stranger, aren't you?"

"No."

"Tell the truth."

"Go home, Cordelia," he ordered. All the joy from sex with her had dwindled down to a distant memory. Fully clothed, verbal armor intact, it was hard to imagine they had coupled at all.

"I told you there was nothing good about that man being in Josephine's house. It's something you just feel."

He opened the door to his bedroom. He pushed her into the hallway. When they got to the top of the faded carpet on the stairs, he wondered what would happen if she fell by accident.

How would he explain the fall? Would she die with her secrets or would she spill them all, out of retaliation? "It's late," he said. "I've got things to do before dark."

She tapped her pocketbook as if she wanted to tap him upside the head with it. If she tapped him on the head, would he hit her back? At that moment, Cordelia was unsure which one of them was more angry with the other. After a few seconds of glaring she said, "Don't rush me."

He dropped his eyes first. She was the only woman he knew who could make him feel like a shrinking man. "We can't afford to fight each other."

"You're saying this because of him," she said, referring to Hannibal.

"Yeah."

"What do you think about the stranger, Grady?" When he would have looked away, she caught his chin with gentle fingers. "The truth."

He kissed her middle fingers, which she pressed against his lips. She cherished this small concession to the anger between them. Since they were pretty much two of a kind, they rarely fought. Besides, there was too much at stake for them to be anything but friends.

The reverend put his hand at the small of her back, then guided her down the carpeted stairs. In the foyer, he spoke the worry on his mind. "I think we're in trouble. Big trouble."

ELEVEN

That evening, Hannibal reclined in peace with Josephine in her living room. A large fire cast a romantic glow over a welcoming space that was as soothing to Hannibal as it was cozy. His voice sounded heavy and rich and satisfied when he said to the woman who held center stage in his thoughts and dreams, "Dinner was great."

The pleasure shining through Josephine's eyes was at odds with the matter-of-fact way she spoke. "It was just red beans and rice."

He chuckled over her understatement; he doubted her tone would have been much different had she been quoting him the sum of two plus two. Once again, she had put her foot in the meal she had prepared for them both, only this time, she had made enough food to serve an uninvited dinner guest. If Cordelia Brennon showed up tonight, there would be food to warm her belly, drink to cool her tongue.

"There was ham in those beans and the

cornbread was half as tall as that apple cake you've got cooling in the kitchen for your neighbor to have tomorrow. I'm stuffed, Josephine."

"No room for vanilla ice cream and oatmeal cookies?"

Hannibal laughed. "I wish I did have room."

With few words, he and Josephine had settled into a quiet domestic scene, a setting complete with after-dinner mint tea on a wicker serving tray. There were tulip-covered paper napkins on the serving tray, two plain white cups with saucers, and a speckled blue teapot.

Hannibal felt delirious with pleasure. He had a tremendous urge to pull his boots off so that he could cross his feet on the coffee table, which is exactly what he would have done in his own home—if he had one.

The scent of apples and cinnamon coming from the cooling cake in Josephine's kitchen bound him to the moment as surely as his curiosity bound his mind to the woman who made him think more and more about settling down for longer than a season.

More and more, Hannibal had the urge to set his roots for a lifetime of home and hearth, and if he was lucky, for a lifetime of love. He was smart enough to realize that Josephine was the reason he considered making so drastic a change in his life.

On one of the rare occasions when he and

Mac Bishop were getting along, Mac had told Hannibal, "Man, you're the ultimate bachelor." Coming from Mac, those were more than big words, those words were a confession of his admiration.

In turn, Hannibal admired Josephine; if he was the ultimate bachelor, she was the ultimate bachelorette. She had it all—her own home, her own hearth, her own business, and most important, she had her own mind. Josephine might be a recluse, but she was a recluse by choice, not by demand.

Her choice disturbed Hannibal's sense of right over wrong. He felt it was right for her to live as a recluse if it made her happy, but he felt she was very unhappy. Why else would she wear the same color day after day, as if it mattered none?

He had yet to see her wear a dominant color other than brown. He had never thought there were so many shades of brown. From tan to dark chocolate, Josephine Brennon wore them all.

Despite the underlying unhappiness that he was sure formed the basis of her don't-give-a-damn attitude, Hannibal admired the way Josephine had found a way to stretch beyond her disfigurement and her unhelpful relatives to be a story of success.

Because she had found a way to reach beyond her own solitude to touch people through the food she prepared with gifted hands, she had also found a way to touch him.

Food.

Hearth.

Home.

In Josephine's hands, flour and shortening and water became flaky crust for pies made of buttermilk, pecan, or creamy sweet potatoes. Salt, pepper, and Louisiana hot sauce were the basic ingredients for the chicken she fried to perfection.

That was Josephine to Hannibal, a basic and uplifting woman, a woman whose company was quiet food for his restless soul. It would have shocked him to discover that it was the very idea of his rambling, of his being a drifter, that appealed most to her.

While Hannibal studied her through half-closed eyes, she thumbed through her latest mail-order cookbook, her eyes not really seeing the printed words or the step-by-step food preparation pictures on the cool, slick pages the cookbook held.

She was busy thinking about him. Of all the primary colors, the one color Josephine associated with Hannibal was the color yellow, her favorite shade in the color spectrum.

Far from a secretive color, yellow was the color of the sun. The sun was light. Light was friendly and extroverted—like Hannibal Ray. In his presence, she almost felt beautiful. Almost.

Her fingers stopped flipping through the mail-order cookbook she had received that afternoon. She stared at Hannibal, her eyes hungry, her soul starved for love.

He recognized the hungry, searching look on her face, a look that forced him to accept his own accountability for the way he had been manipulating her since he'd kissed her in the kitchen.

He had gone out of his way to win her trust by defending her. He had made it a point to her and to anybody who threatened her safety or peace of mind that he was a force to be reckoned with on her behalf.

The hungry, needy look in Josephine's unguarded moment revealed to Hannibal that he had at last scratched the façade of her cool demeanor. Her cavalier attitude had challenged him, and he had fought her don't-give-a-damn ways with deliberate courtship. Now—he drew a deep breath—now, he had to ask himself how far he was prepared to go with her.

He knew he was leaving; now or later, he was leaving. He knew their having a future together was as unlikely as Cordelia Brennon waltzing through the front door with a smile on her habitually pinched lips.

How far did he want to go with Josephine, this tragic, haunting young woman whose virginal oneness made him feel humble and strong at the same time?

How far?

The answer came to him without fanfare. He would pursue Josephine until the hereafter. This knowledge trapped Hannibal in Destiny as surely as it challenged him to live or die in his quest to win Josephine's heart.

On the surface, his answer made no real sense, not based on the short time he had known her in the flesh. But Hannibal felt as if some part of his soul had known Josephine since before time.

Maybe his being in Destiny was not simply symbolic of life in time-present, but symbolic in terms of life in time-infinity. It was a logical way for him to explain the oneness in her which seemed to fit the emptiness in him. Why else would he feel the urge to stop drifting from season to season between Texas and the Dakotas?

Just as the dinner of beans and rice had filled him, Josephine's spirit had filled him. That her spirit was troubled gave him purpose, a direction to take in the uncharted territory of her private universe.

By being a recluse, she opposed his nomad's way of thinking. She curbed his urban wandering, at least for now. Right now, Hannibal could no more run from his desire to cherish her idiosyncrasies than he could run from his goal to liberate her from being alone and lonely in a farmhouse that was slowly, gracefully falling into decline.

What force held her to the home she treated as a shrine? Was it love, was it hate, or was it the feeling that somehow, some way, she was incomplete? Like him, had she been waiting for someone to fill her void?

Hannibal returned Josephine's look of hunger with one of solemnity. Now that he had her trust, it was time to reinforce that trust with facts. He needed facts to successfully fight her enemies. Specifically, those enemies were Reverend Franklin, Sister Shirley Louise, Sister Bea, and Cordelia Brennon.

Since the very formidable Cordelia Brennon led the list of Josephine's enemies, Hannibal decided she was the one person he needed to help Josephine conquer; not conquer by force, or even by love, but by Josephine's will to live her own good life on her own good terms. That was the way he lived as a drifter—by his own means, in his own good time.

The facts, Hannibal repeated in his mind like a mantra. He needed the facts, but also he needed to be careful not to alienate Josephine because of his own self-centered manipulations.

Like Cordelia Brennon, he had his own agenda when it came to Josephine, and like Cordelia Brennon's, his agenda was an undeclared threat to Josephine's peace of mind. Yes, Hannibal wanted to free Josephine from the farmhouse, but he also wanted to free her to come to him, only him, always him—until kingdom come.

Hannibal herded his wits together. He used his wits to build the strategy he needed to win his goal: an uninhibited Josephine. Yet he was the outsider in the drama being played out in the Brennon household. He needed an advantage.

The advantage he had over Cordelia Brennon was that being an outsider meant he had the weapon of objectivity on his side. There was no history to tamper with his single-minded mission to win Josephine's troubled heart. *Get the facts,* he reminded himself, *the facts.*

"Josephine?"

"Hmm?"

"How did your Aunt Cordelia know you made smothered chicken the first night I came here? There were only two place settings at the supper table. She made it plain you hadn't called her."

Josephine thought of the retired electrician who raised fish bait he sold at a nearby lake well-known for its bluegill and bass. "The guy I bartered greens for chicken told her. He's her neighbor."

Hannibal laughed. "I've spent a big part of my life moving from one small town to another, and yet it still amazes me how quickly news travels from one house to the next."

"Why don't you settle in a big city?"

"Big cities have too many people going too fast. I guess I'm a country boy at heart. There's something almost grand about miles of rough country road."

She tossed her new cookbook on top of the stack on the floor beside her chair. He had her total attention. "I don't find bad road appealing."

He searched his mind for a way to make her understand. "Out on the road, I see time standing still, Josephine."

"How do you mean?"

"I see wheat growing wild, open sky, millions of stars, strange birds. I like the way trees and wildlife change from one side of a state to the other. I like the hospitality of people who live miles apart and are glad to see a fresh face. I like seeing working farms and knowing that most of the food we eat in the States comes from the States. Out on the road, I see continuity."

"Continuity?"

"Yeah. The American Dream. Freedom. Apple pie from scratch. Pickled peaches. I don't know if I'll ever get tired of traveling cross-country at my own pace."

Josephine had to remind herself that despite all the romance she heard in his voice, Hannibal had been homeless until she gave him a home. He had arrived on her doorstep *alive*, not just comfortable in his own skin, but excited about what might happen next. Next, as in the future, as in hope.

"You like measuring time by the season and not by the hour, don't you, Hannibal?"

"Yeah, I guess I do."

After several companionable moments, she eased their conversation around a more personal corner. "What about your family?"

He was pleased she asked. "You already know I don't have a wife or kids stashed away somewhere. I've got two brothers and a sister. Grayson is a bull rider and travels as much as I do, which is probably why he never married either. Kipp trains rescue teams to save lives in disaster situations, like the bombing at the World Trade Center in New York and the bombing at the Murrah Building in Oklahoma City. He's married and lives in Texas, just a couple of hours from our sister, Dorrie. Dorrie still lives with my mom in Half Dead, Texas. They are the main reason I ever go back home."

Coming from a small town, Josephine knew many of them were given names that seemed funny based on contemporary standards of judging. "Home is Half Dead?"

Home. Hannibal remembered his last fight with Mac Bishop and his failed relationship with Rosalie Jones. Mac and Rosalie were two stabilizing forces in Half Dead: one for good, the other for mischief. Aside from his sister's family and his mother, Mac and Rosalie were two of the most interesting people Hannibal knew in Half Dead. Half Dead was his hometown, but it was not his home.

He finally answered, "Yeah."

"Tell me about it."

"There's nothing to tell."

Josephine disagreed; everybody had a story to tell. "What about your grandmother? When you talk about her I can tell you were crazy about her."

"She died young."

"Go on."

Normally, Hannibal shared few details about his private life. Doing so now felt right. "Her name was Clarabelle. Most people called her Belle. Me and my brothers and sister called her Big Mama."

"On your dad or your mom's side?"

"My dad's. We spent a lot of time with Big Mama when we were growing up. Mostly the summers. That's when she did her pickling. Big Mama pickled everything from eggs to peaches. I loved the pickled peaches most because she made 'em spicy. When my parents weren't around, she let me eat peaches by the jar if I wanted to. Big Mama was great."

"You said she died young?"

"Throat cancer. Big Mama smoked unfiltered cigarettes until she couldn't smoke 'em anymore. My dad died of cancer from smoking. I hate tobacco of any kind."

"I don't blame you. How about your mom?"

"Like I said, she lives with my sister and her family."

"Do you see them much?"

"I see them mostly during the big holidays of the summer. I haven't missed the Fourth of July or Labor Day with my mom in ten years."

Josephine seldom celebrated holidays herself. It seemed like a bother for just one person, although she decorated her home for Thanksgiving and for Christmas. "I'd think you'd do the cold-season holidays with your mother and sister."

"I'm usually bunked down for the winter somewhere like I am now. Besides, those are family holidays."

This was the first time Josephine heard sadness in his voice. "Your mother and sister are your family. The way your voice sounds when you talk about them shows you've got a pretty good relationship with them."

"I guess I quit going for Thanksgiving and Easter for the same reason I quit going for Christmas. I don't have any kids or a house or a wife or a big corporate job or anything else to brag about. They think I'm a loser."

"I don't."

"Then you're an exception."

Before he finished talking, Josephine was already shaking her head. Hannibal had too much confidence to be a loser. "No. I think it's great you don't feel the need to answer to anybody. You are your own man."

Her feisty position pleased him. Still, he said, "After a while though, people start measuring a man by the things he owns and not by who he is. I own my truck and pretty much the clothes on my back."

"Freedom."

She sounded so wistful, he asked a personal question of his own. "Why don't you leave Destiny, Josephine?"

It was as if a concrete wall appeared in front of them out of nowhere. She stopped being friendly. "Nobody wants a scarred woman."

This time he was the one shaking his head before she could finish talking. "Your scar is not a disability."

Self-conscious, she turned the scarred side of her face away from him. "I'm ugly."

The scar was only part of the whole that made her a woman. She had good bones, healthy skin, and gorgeous hair. Her figure was trim, her hips and breasts the very size Hannibal liked to hold in his hands. "Not to me."

The sensuality in his voice made her skin tingle with physical awareness. "Don't, Hannibal."

She saw that his muscles were coiled for action, as if at any moment he might surge to his stocking feet, pull her into his arms and . . . Josephine pressed her palm against her scarred cheek. She was ugly, pitifully ugly. It was she who surged to her feet, she who lost control. "Don't!"

It took every ounce of Hannibal's will to keep from snatching her palm away from her face. She had no reason to hide from him. If he had his way, before the winter season was done, she would have no secrets from him at all, not one.

"Don't what?" he said coldly. "Don't say I want to kiss you again? That I don't want to take that stupid red band off your hair? You've got beautiful hair, Josephine. *You* are beautiful."

"Liar!" The word rasped harshly from her throat. Josephine's temper, shielded by a cavalier attitude honed by years of Cordelia Brennon's verbal abuse, had come quickly in response to his assertion that her scar could be ignored.

Her temper had come quickly all right, to the flash point of violence even, but she was not the only angry soul in the fire-lit living room with its speckled blue pot filled with cold mint tea. Hannibal was as mad at Josephine as she was at him.

"I never lie."

She snarled like a cornered cat. "All men are liars!"

Her passion, deep and unbridled, was a serious turn-on for Hannibal. She was not as cool and nonchalant as she would have him believe. It made her more approachable, less like the untouched virgin her life depicted.

Whether or not she had ever had sex before

was irrelevant to him. She still lived a virgin's life, seemingly untouched by the outside world. He wanted to be the man to open her eyes to the joys she was missing on the great open road he never tired of exploring.

He wanted . . . to make her understand that his opinion of her was not dictated by the scar on her face; he wanted to love her, not pity her. "How would you know about all men?" he demanded. "When was the last time you left this house, let alone Destiny?"

She had the urge to kick him. "That's none of your business."

Oh, how he begged to differ. "You made it my business the day you hired me. Cordelia made it my business when she barged in here to boss you around for nothing, when she sent her buddies to bully you."

"Be quiet."

He had no intention of being ordered around, not by Cordelia, not by the reverend, not by the woman shooting bullets at him through her eyes. He spoke in a low, angry voice. "I want to know what makes you tick, Josephine Brennon."

"Quiet!"

"No, I won't be quiet." His crotch was as stiff as an iron poker and she couldn't care less if he lived or died. *Damn her.* Damn her for making him care too much too soon.

She returned to her seat across from him.

"Yes, you will." Her words were hard chips of ice.

Hannibal's eyes narrowed at her implied statement that she was so tough she needed no one. "You can handle it when people treat you like crap, but when somebody treats you good, you run away from it."

He leaned his body over the coffee table, one hand on either side of the wicker serving tray. "Why is that, Josephine? Why are you running from me now, when you should have been slamming the door in my face instead of hiring me? You don't know me, but you let me work for you. Defend you. You feed me and treat me so damn good I'll be hard-pressed to leave when spring comes, and yet you refuse to be treated with kindness yourself."

She refused to listen to a man she was close to firing. He had no right to criticize the way she lived. "Get out."

"No."

"I said get out."

She was solidified carbon dioxide: dry ice. For the first time, Hannibal saw the family resemblance Josephine bore to Cordelia Brennon. The resemblance was in the shape of the head, the stubborn set of the chin, the haughty turn of the eye, the kiss-my-butt attitude.

Josephine's pristine passion was the kind of passion that could bring him to his knees. She was tough, but Hannibal was tougher. If getting fired was the price for speaking his mind, then so be it. "You deserve to be treated with respect."

The fact he felt he had to say such a thing at all clued him in to how skewed and out of touch Josephine was when it came to interpersonal relationships, with men or women. He did not need to be in touch with his feminine self to know this. He only needed to be human.

If Cordelia Brennon had been Josephine's solitary role model, then Hannibal reasoned he might be taking on a woman who was a lot more complicated than he expected to take on. The increased stakes upped his desire for the prize: Josephine's heart.

He was ready to take her on in any test of wills she presented to him. The thought, *Winners never quit and quitters never win* crossed his strategy-building mind.

Let her fight all she wanted to fight. He could take it, and besides, she needed the reality check. Living alone the way she did, spoiled by her own self-contained lifestyle, Josephine had a thing or two to learn about not getting her own way. Let her be pissed off; let her skin flush and her eyes shine just for him.

Let her come ALIVE.

She braced her arms on the lightly cluttered coffee table and got right into his taunting, handsome face. "Don't you dare preach to me, Hannibal Ray. I get enough preaching from the reverend."

They were nose-to-nose. "What about guidance, Josephine? How long have you lived in this house alone?"

He had stepped way over the line of propriety. He was arrogant, immovable, and sexy as hell. He had a will strong enough to match her own. Even though she hated what she was hearing, Josephine did like the way he spoke his mind.

She reciprocated the gesture. "I'm not a child. How I live is none of your business."

"You told me that in a small town everything is everybody's business. I don't care about everybody. I care about you."

She scowled at him. "That's impossible."

"No, you are impossible."

She reacted as if her face had been slapped—eyes wide, mouth open in shocked dismay. "What?"

He sat back from the table and glared at her. If he was going to get fired, at least it would be on a full stomach and with full peace of mind. He was not leaving town until he told her it was past time she got a life. "You want to be a victim."

Why did he have to say victim? She despised that word. She had carved herself a life that had nothing to do with that word. Scar or no scar, one thing she had plenty of was pride. "No way am I a victim."

"Prove it."

She kicked a leg on the coffee table. Clearly, she wanted to kick him. "I don't have to prove anything to you."

He relaxed his voice, but not his opposition. "You do need to prove something to yourself."

"Since you know me so well after one hot second, tell me. Tell me what I need to prove."

"You need to prove you can do more than survive. You need to prove you can thrive, Josephine."

She smacked her hand on the coffee table. The cups rattled against the saucers. Mint tea splashed on the wicker tray. "By running all over the state in a raggedy truck with a box in the back full of clothes the way you do?"

She had a good point.

So did he. "At least I'm free."

She stared at him without blinking. She stared a hole straight through him, but she held her tongue.

"I'm not scared of you, Josephine."

She leaned back. She crossed her legs. She clasped her hands in her lap. She forced a serene mask into place; they might have been discussing the weather for all the polite calm she portrayed. "Maybe you should be scared."

Oh, how her self-control turned him on. The control turned him on because he knew she was mad enough to chuck the dishes into the fireplace. Hannibal felt so intense, so moved, he wound up speaking the truth. "I'm scared of the way I feel about you, Josephine. It's strong. *You* are strong. Wherever you are is where I want to be."

The man was spectacular. He had no secretive thoughts in his mind. She tried not to ask but she did ask—in a whisper. "Why are you saying these things?"

"I think of you constantly."

She knew the scar was not what he thought about. His entire body language showed he was as interested in what she had to say as he was in the way she chose to say it.

She just could not figure out what she had that could turn a traveling man like him on. She wore her hair the same way every day. She dressed for comfort instead of style. She wore no perfume. "I can't imagine why."

"In another woman, I might think you were fishing for compliments, but you aren't like any other woman I know."

"Bastard."

"I'm not talking about the X on your face."

"Yes, you are! Just say it. Say it!" She picked up a dish from the table and flung it to the wall. "I'm ugly!"

"Josephine."

In one long swing, she cleared every dish from the coffee table. "Ugly!"

"Josephine."

She grabbed a thick crystal candleholder

from the end table at her right elbow. She took aim at the single mirror in the living room.

He grabbed her wrist. "No."

She had stopped seeing him, stopped hearing a word he said. She was too caught up in the idea that he pitied her. She wanted none of his pity. She wanted his good opinion. "Get out! Out!"

He stayed where he was, but it was hard, so very hard. "I can't, baby. I'm in way too deep to turn back now."

She was in deeper than he was because it was her living room they were fighting in. He was a stranger, but it felt right for him to stand beside her. She felt as if he was the missing link to her own self, and even while this thought thrilled her, it scared her too.

She spent too much time alone with her thoughts and needs to pretend she had no idea where he was coming from when it came to their chemistry together. "Why, Hannibal? Why me?"

"I can't stop thinking about you because you're one of a kind. I want to take care of you, Josephine. We'd be good for each other."

"After knowing each other less than two months?"

Kindred spirits dealt with emotions. When kindred spirits united, there was no void. In Josephine's home, Hannibal felt far from empty. He felt connected to a higher power and that power was love.

"I've been searching for something or someone special my whole life. Now, I know why I could never keep still. I had to find you."

Josephine looked stricken, shell-shocked. "You can't want me, Hannibal. Nobody wants me."

"I do."

"I don't want your pity!"

This time he did shake her. When he was done, when her hair was wild around her head, he kissed her until her legs turned to jelly. He kissed her until she broke down and cried.

He wiped away her tears with his thumbs. "I wish I could say I was sorry, but I'm not. If I thought you'd let me carry you up those stairs, I would do it. I want to make love to you, Josephine, but only when you're ready."

"You're leaving."

"Not any time soon."

"I'm not a diversion."

He laughed softly. "You're too complicated to be a diversion."

"Thanks."

"You're welcome."

She pulled away and he let her go.

Hannibal watched her intently, and was not surprised his heart ached for her. She climbed the stairs alone to her bed day after day, night after night, and this night would be no exception. On this cold winter evening, she climbed the stairs completely humbled, the flat of one palm pressed gently against the scar on her face.

Hannibal's long body was taut with suppressed energy. The urge to go to her, to do nothing more than hold her safe in his powerful arms, required all his common sense to keep him in his place. He was a hired hand, a drifter, and come spring, Josephine Brennon would be a mystery that could easily remain unsolved.

TWELVE

The Brennon Farmhouse
Three Weeks Later
4:20 PM

In the kitchen, Josephine studied the gingerbread recipe she had perfected. The four-by-five inch card she held in her hand read:

Gingerbread

$^1/_2$ *cup white sugar*
1 cup light molasses
$^3/_4$ *cup butter*
$^1/_2$ *teaspoon cinnamon*
$^1/_2$ *teaspoon cloves*
1 teaspoon fresh ginger (or to taste)
1 teaspoon baking soda
2 $^1/_2$ cups flour
1 cup hot water
2 eggs

In a large bowl, combine sugar and butter until creamy. Add eggs, molasses, and water and beat until smooth. Add dry ingredients and mix well. Pour into 10 x 13 inch rectangle pan. Bake on 350° for 30-40 minutes. Serve warm with vanilla ice cream on the side.

Josephine scanned the recipe one more time. She grabbed the dry ingredients from the shelves to make the recipe, then realized she had no true desire to bake anything; she had a headache the size of Nebraska. The ingredients went back on the shelves, the recipe back in its box on the kitchen counter.

She knew the headache was from the rubber band she wore every day to keep her ponytail in place. To ease the soreness of her scalp, she loosened the band so that there was a pucker of hair between the band and her skull. It felt better.

Still massaging her scalp with one hand, she gazed with unfocused eyes outside the kitchen window. She felt miserable, and not just because of her aching head.

She was thinking about the distance she had placed between herself and Hannibal after the night she knocked the dishes from the coffee table in her living room. Since then, they had been strictly professional. If their relationship went beyond business, it was up to her to make it happen.

Every time Josephine thought about that night, she felt like a fool. Hannibal wanted to make her happy, yet she pushed him away. Because of her attraction to him, he could easily seduce her into his bed. Instead, he made her wonder about what she was missing. Now, kissing was no longer enough.

In the weeks since she had climbed the stairs alone to her bedroom, her hand pressed against the mark on her face, she realized something important about Hannibal Ray: He had true honor.

Perhaps he felt it was wrong to have sex with her when he knew her emotions were . . . confused. Soon he would leave Destiny. When he was gone, she would be more lonely than ever before. Sex would further complicate her already complex life. She doubted she would find another man she admired more than Hannibal.

The urge to go to him, to ask him to take her away from Destiny, was a powerful one. When he left, and she knew he would leave soon, what did she have to offer him? Nothing. Everything she owned, including her identity, was confined to the Brennon farm.

If she left Destiny with Hannibal, would their love be enough to sustain them? Did she have the nerve to try? She wanted to try, but she was scared and too proud to explain to him why she felt bound to the Brennon farm. She would have to reveal her secrets.

He would think she was crazy.

All her armor for self-protection was fast eroding under Hannibal's constant regard. His attention to her needs was faultless. It was almost as if he had come to Destiny to show her just how tiny and uneventful her sheltered life had been all these many years.

Today, she felt a terrible sadness.

Tears came to her eyes, but never fell. She chose the way she lived; if suddenly she felt she had wasted part of her life, it was her own fault. Every time she looked at Hannibal she imagined he thought she was a coward. She hated for him to think so little of her.

Josephine covered her face with her hands. Tears were locked in her throat. She almost choked from the tears stacking up inside her, but she refused to give in to the urge to wallow in self-pity.

She had created her environment. If she wanted a deeper relationship with Hannibal, it was up to her to bring about the change needed to make it happen. The winter season was nearing its end and the clock was ticking; she was running out of time.

With her face covered, Josephine failed to see Hannibal open the door to his cottage, neither did she see him study her through the open curtains of the kitchen window near the dining table that was set for no one. He came to the kitchen door quietly. His knock was soft.

In a panic, Josephine yanked off the rubber band, smoothed her hair into place with her hands, and put the band back on. She opened the door, but just a crack. "Yeah?"

"Let's take a walk around the property. I'd like you to see the changes I've made."

"We can do it later."

His eyes were dark, inscrutable pools of humanity. "Were you crying Josephine?"

"No. I . . . I have a headache."

"Why don't you sit down for a while. I'll pick some of the mint out in the garden here and make you some tea."

He was offering her friendship. She desperately needed a friend. She opened the door all the way. "About that walk?" Josephine asked.

"Yes."

"I'd love to."

He was relieved. "Good."

She watched him step into the kitchen. Dressed in his Stetson, sheepskin coat, Lee jeans, and boots, Hannibal looked huge and forbidding. Josephine wished she had the nerve to burrow beneath his coat, her face pressed against his chest, her arms around his waist. Had she asked, she knew he would have welcomed her. She said breathlessly, "I'll get my jacket."

"And while you're at it, maybe you should take your hair down. It might ease your headache."

"My hair is so long and heavy it gets on my neck and ears and makes me feel hot."

"It's cold outside. Your hair ought to feel good around your face."

"I know, but—"

He held up a hand to ward off an argument. "That's okay. I just thought you'd be more comfortable." He touched her face with his eyes. "You have beautiful hair, Josephine. I hope to see you wear it down someday soon."

She felt giddy, absolutely giddy. One minute ago she had the blues, and now she felt ready to use the wind to fly. "I'll be right back." She ran from the kitchen to grab her coat from the closet off the foyer.

Hannibal waited at the kitchen door. Carefully, he kept his mind blank. The chemistry between them was a steady, sensual burn he had to temper with common sense.

With her long, heavy hair and her huge, tear-stained eyes, she drew him into her turbulent world in a way he feared would eventually run so deep it would be everlasting.

Destiny.

Time-infinity.

Until kingdom come.

They walked through the kitchen door into the dormant garden. In the garden, he had turned the ground over where it was bare and improved its quality by adding topsoil. When it came time for spring planting, Josephine's herbs and vegetables would taste better than the year before.

He next led her to the front yard. He had painted the porch rails and reinforced the trellis that supported the climbing yellow rosebush, now dormant and free of its early winter blooms.

As Josephine studied his handiwork, she heard the latch at the gate open. It was as if a freight train thundered over her heart. The sound of the latch moving open made her forget her headache; Hannibal wanted to walk *outside* the property. No way was she going outside. She stared at the latch on the gate as if she had never seen it before.

"Josephine?"

"I've changed my mind," she said in a rush. "Mint tea sounds great. I'll get the kettle boiling."

Hannibal closed the gate. With heavy steps, he approached her. With tender fingers, he lifted her chin. The desperate look in her eyes broke him down. Sweet God, she was beautiful. "Come here, baby. Come here."

She burrowed beneath his jacket, her face pressed hard against his chest. In his arms, Josephine forgot all about passing busybodies who might report to Aunt Cordelia about her carrying on with the handyman on the front lawn.

She forgot everything but how good it felt to be treated with love and respect. She never wanted Hannibal to let her go, but in the end, it was she who pulled away. "Thank you."

"I like holding you, Josephine. You don't ever need to thank me for doing something I'd do all day long if you'd only let me."

"I want you to hold me too, Hannibal, but I'm afraid."

"I wouldn't hurt you."

"No." She shuddered from the cold she clung to within. "I'd be the one hurting you."

"Don't worry about me. I know what I want."

He wanted everything, body and soul, but she was still unready. "I don't have the strength yet to leave this place and I have no right to ask you to stay longer than the winter repairs. Let's be friends. At least, let us have that much."

A slash of pain, like lightning, cut across Hannibal's temple. Was this how frustrated Rosalie had been with him when he left town thinking they would always be "just friends"?

He wanted a whole lot more than friendship from Josephine. He wanted to join her in the cottage bed where he dreamed so often of making love to her. He wanted to be with her for . . . how long?

He was no further today with Josephine than he had been on the night she swept the dishes from coffee table onto the living room floor.

How long would it take before her claustrophobic lifestyle drove him straight up a wall? Spring would be no problem, but summer would come and it would be hot, the kind of weather that made him want to be on the road. Maybe Josephine was right. Maybe they should settle on friendship, settle on . . . tea.

"You start the kettle boiling, Josephine. I'll pick the mint leaves for brewing. For some reason, that mint won't give in to the season."

She placed a hand on the sheepskin covering his arm. His arm felt tense, harder than the native red rock the town of Destiny was built on. "I'm sorry, Hannibal."

"So am I."

But oh, how she enchanted him. Food, clothing, shelter, and prosperity were all challenges she had not only conquered but mastered in her limited world. She was humble in manner, soft-spoken. She never rambled on and on to fill gaps of peaceful silence between them.

Beneath that gentle, modest façade, she was tough. Her living arrangement was tragic to him because in Destiny, there was no man who appreciated her strength the way he did.

Hannibal knew there was no significant man in her life, because if she had one, the man would be there to serve and protect her. A woman as strong beneath the surface as Josephine was would expect no less.

In turn, Josephine appreciated the way Hannibal allowed her to be herself. He took her moods and her lifestyle in stride, for which she was thankful. He could easily have made a big issue about her not leaving the yard to tour the property.

He had chosen instead to provide her with the comfort and shelter of his arms during a time when she felt like a total idiot. It had been one more episode that made her face the stark fact she was fully grown and more than a little bit neurotic.

Other than her unwillingness to open the latch to her gate and walk outside the property line, she was a practical woman governed by sensible feelings. She had no illusions about how bleak her future would be after Hannibal was gone.

She was as direct and honest about her life as he was about his life. He had the skills to settle down, but he had no desire to settle down. He could own more than a truck, but he had no need for more than a truck. He was who he was and he made no apologies; neither did she. In this way, they were two of a kind.

They both were willing to sacrifice their all to keep their individuality. She wanted to live, and maybe, just maybe, Hannibal wanted something to live for. It was the details of change that were causing them problems. She knew this as surely as she felt her headache going away.

She said, "I've got some honey to go with that tea."

"No cookies?" he teased.

"Not a one."

"Good. I thought you cooked all the time."

She laughed, something she did a lot now that Hannibal was there with her. "No, I just have goodies around most of the time. Every now and then I run out of something common, like vanilla extract or eggs, and I'm not able to cook something I had in mind to cook. Sometimes, like today, I don't feel like cooking at all."

He felt honored. Today, she was letting down her guard a tad more. "How about a fire to go with that tea?"

She smiled. Hannibal had a way of making her wish she had colors in her closet that were not overshadowed by black or brown. Right now she wished she wore red instead of brown and that she had the courage to do something different about her hair.

"I'm going to run upstairs and . . . put my coat away," she said, although she knew she was going to do just a little bit more. There was nothing she could do on short notice about her wardrobe, but she could do something about her hair. "I'll meet you in the living room. Nobody has served me tea before."

Excited as a schoolboy to know his gift of time and patience pleased her, he grinned like a fool. So what if they never went anywhere together? For the first time, Hannibal Ray was learning to be satisfied with living in the moment.

When Josephine returned to the living room, her long and beautiful hair in a French braid down her back, the tail of the braid looped and tied with a red satin ribbon, he fell hopelessly, irrevocably in love.

They sat in her living room until dawn. The fire had burned to embers and had been re-kindled several times during the night. They had spoken of the books they each had read, the movies they had watched. There was no mention of any problems, past or present. It was a satisfying experience for them both.

The last of the mint tea Hannibal had pre-pared, along with the cold cuts Josephine had eventually put together, were long since gone. Yet for them, time still moved with ease, their bodies a long way from feeling tired.

The presence of one rejuvenated the other until each felt fortified, sustained by the truth and beauty that was the beginning of any re-lationship built to last through time.

Until . . . Kingdom . . . Come.

Hannibal moved them into another deeper, more intimate level of communication when he said, "I'll make breakfast." The very sound of his statement smacked of commitment.

She blew out the light from a smoldering candle, the resulting smoke moving through her cozy living room with the ease of unno-ticed danger. Flames were life itself, smoke the death of life.

By all that made sense, Josephine mused, she should feel afraid of the man who entered her life as a handyman, only to destroy the

safe world she had so meticulously put together.

By allowing him to use the most personal
room in her house, the kitchen, she knew she
was actually binding herself to him. For
Josephine, this was a moment of reckoning, a
moment of no turning back.

If she allowed Hannibal to cook in her
kitchen, she would be giving him access to an
intimate piece of herself, a piece of her private
sanctuary. What if she were wrong about his
integrity? What if she was doing herself more
harm than good?

If ever there was a time to trust her instincts,
this was one of those times. After all, she reasoned, a man's hands did not lie. Hannibal's
hands were used to hard work, were clean and
clipped along the nails, and he used lotion,
the mark of a man who cared about himself.
A man who cared about himself in such a
small, almost unnoticeable way had room to
care for others.

Josephine watched the meandering smoke
from the single melted candle wind its way
through the air until the smoke disappeared
into nothingness, until she realized nothingness was sometimes a welcome state of being.
It was a welcome state because she felt no danger. She felt no fear.

Life after death.

Destiny.

Her heart soared in this moment of truth.

She wanted him in her kitchen, in her bed, in her arms. "So, what is your breakfast specialty, Mr. Hannibal Ray?"

His relief at being asked this question lessened the tension in his broad, muscular shoulders, and rushed more joy through his veins. "Cheese omelets, bacon, and toast."

"I've got eggs but no cheese, Jimmy Dean sausage, and plain bagels for bread."

His smile was everything nice, his heart not on his sleeve, but in the way he carried himself. He carried himself with pride, with dignity, and with compassion for the woman who just shared with him the past twelve hours of his life.

He had a feeling that those twelve hours of spiritual and emotional saturation would ground them during the troubling days that were sure to come. The winter season was coming to an end, and still there had been no vow of commitment between them. Josephine was still unready. He said, "Sounds good to me."

As the couple prepared their morning meal, Josephine marveled at how synchronized they moved around her kitchen. It was as if he belonged in her feel-good space. She said, "I can't believe how fast the time went by."

"I can."

She sniffed the air near the frying pan, its center filled with eggs seasoned with plain salt and pepper. Her stomach growled at the sight.

"Mmm," she complimented him, "everything smells great." She opened a cupboard to the right of the stainless steel kitchen sink. "Why don't I set the table while you finish up here?"

"Go for it." He cleared his throat, full now with feelings that ran deeper than pure desire. He cast about for something neutral to say. "What about juice?"

She breezed by him, silverware in hand. "Never drink the stuff."

He stacked the sausage on one side of a heavy, blue, stoneware dinner plate, golden eggs on the other. "Who doesn't drink juice for breakfast?"

"I drink water or ginger ale for breakfast. I don't like milk, which is why there's no cheese in the fridge. I never could stand the stuff even though I cook with it all the time."

"Ginger ale it is, then."

She picked a bottle of raspberry-flavored ginger ale from the pantry, set it on the counter, and pulled ice cubes from the freezer for their water goblets. The kitchen was totally silent except for the sounds of cooking. The domestic scene made her heart thump rapidly. "I've never had a man cook breakfast in my kitchen before."

A surge of possessive energy coursed through Hannibal. In his experience, a woman's kitchen was the heart of her home. His basic problem with Josephine was that she refused to leave her front yard. Even if he lived in Destiny, he could never be completely happy confined to six acres of land.

Hannibal grinned. "I feel honored."

She grinned back. "You should."

He eased her chair away from the table before sitting across from her, a cream stoneware vase filled with dried sunflowers between them.

On the surface, Hannibal shared breakfast with a woman he found profoundly interesting. He had reached an exquisite destination in life. The reaching of this sacred place of renewal expressed itself through his actions. Without any flourish or fanfare, he poured the first sip of raspberry ginger ale into Josephine's water goblet before filling his own.

This first social grace, this tending first to the needs of another human being, was certain to be a cornerstone of their relationship, necessary if they were to be at least friends after the winter season.

"I want to make mad, passionate love to you," he admitted, "but I figure that won't get me where I really want to go with you right now."

She lifted her water goblet to her lips, savored the first sip of the liquid it held against her tongue, and allowed the bubbles to burst and dissolve before she latched on to her half of their conversation.

"And where is that?"

"A justice of the peace."

Her lids were half closed, the smile on her

face a smile of mystery and romance. "What?" she teased, "No wine? No roses?"

"You are the wine." He lifted his crystal goblet in a toast. "I'll bring the roses."

She studied him then, her eyes wide, her breath swept far, far away by the sheer wonder of finding such treasure in Hannibal. His face was friendly and relaxed. Each movement of his big body was as casual as if he had no place in the universe he would rather be than sitting in her kitchen, eating her food, sharing her life.

He topped the morning with the kindest compliment she thought a man could give a woman who had not seen a mirror in two hours. "You look great first thing in the morning."

She had to laugh. Breaking her sausage in half, she swirled the broken piece in warm maple syrup until she saw him wince at the final result. "If I do, it's only because I don't wear any makeup, so you pretty much see me looking the same way I do every day."

"Maybe. But maybe it's because you're happy."

She felt giddy in the presence of a man who seduced her mind instead of her body. Handsome, solid, and dashing, his look reminded her of Clark Gable in *Gone With the Wind*.

Like Rhett Butler, Hannibal was a man's man and a woman's dream as he refreshed her stagnant, quietly successful life. He had made her cup after cup of mint tea, a time honored act of sharing between friends, an act that showed good will for the present as well as for the future.

She declined comment on her state of happiness; it was a fragile thing. At any moment Cordelia could come crashing in, or the reverend or the sisters might stop by for a little visit and the chance for more buttermilk pie.

Instead of talking about happiness, she reveled in it. It was a beautiful, cold, clear day. The novelty of spending the entire night with an eligible man appealed to her sense of adventure.

This was a man of few apologies, the kind of man who barged through closed doors and other barriers, rebuilt himself by changing his way of living to suit the circumstances in which he found himself—like being a handyman for a reclusive woman. Would he rebuild both their lives? Did she want him to try?

She said, "You tell me you want to make love to me, but you don't so much as kiss even one of my fingers."

"So, you like my kisses?"

"You know what I mean."

She could not dismiss how very different this man was from any other man she had ever seen or read about. Alone with Hannibal, away from prying eyes and listening ears, she saw the intricate, driven being he kept hidden from the rest of the world. Despite his casual ways, this was no casual man. She felt powerless to resist him. "You might be too much for me."

"You're no wallflower yourself."

No man had ever spoken to Josephine the way this man did. The tender way he touched her filled her with an aching sense of wonder at the rarity of her find.

More than a gentleman, more than a handsome face, he was curt and silent, bold and demanding, a bridge from an increasingly desolate present to a promising future. He was an uncommon thief of hearts, a man with a silver tongue.

Of all the men she had seen in classic films or read about in classic books, this man was the king of seduction. She felt as if her clothes were falling off.

This was no young buck in search of himself. This was a man who knew exactly who he was and what he wanted in life, and were it not for the fact that he was a drifter, he would be a man for keeps.

"I'm scared, Hannibal."

"So am I."

"Nothing scares you."

"I'm afraid you're gonna let me walk out of here when spring comes."

His Harry Belafonte voice made her skin quiver in sensual response. "I wish I could say I'll run off with you to the judge, but . . . there are things you don't know about me."

"I know I love you."

Her pulse stumbled, then galloped to life. "Granted, we've been locked up in this house for twelve hours, but—"

"Thirteen hours, five minutes, and thirty-two seconds," he corrected. "I meant just what I said."

Josephine put a hand to her head. All this talk of love made no sense to her, no sense at all. "I've heard love is blind. I've heard spur-of-the-moment romances never last. It's infatuation we've got going on," she argued. "It's just sex more than likely. It's just—"

He put a finger over her mouth. She had said "we" and not "you." She felt the same way he did, at least he hoped she felt the same way he did.

"Don't panic, Josephine. If nothing else, I've proven I can wait until you're ready for whatever move we make next. As far as sex goes, yeah, I want it, but I'm not worried about it. We'll get to it when the time is right. We already know we'll be good together."

Her toes tingled. "Because of the way I fell apart in your arms that time you kissed me in the kitchen? I still can't believe I wrapped my legs around you the way I did."

"Not only that," he countered, "but also because we have great conversation. After a while, sex is just sex, but having things in common, finding pleasure in each other during slow times, is what builds a lasting relationship. I'm after the long haul, Josephine."

She threw him a fastball in order to test his resolve. "What about a family? Would you want your children growing up with a mother with such an ugly scar on her face?"

"Children adapt. As long as we love them right, they won't care what anybody thinks, Josephine. You'll make a great mother."

He saw the heat in her eyes, the tremble of her fingers, and he wanted to hold her in his arms. Yet he was determined to seduce her with his words, to prove to her their destiny had everything to do with love and not lust.

He hit her then with a deadly weapon: his secret fantasy, the one fantasy he had shared with no other woman, not even Rosalie. "Think girls, Josephine. I want baby daughters who have hair and skin and eyes like yours."

His words knocked the wind right out of her. She was hot, hotter than three-digit weather with no clouds in the sky or cool water to drink. "I need one of those big paper fans like the kind you get in church when the weather is so hot you don't think you can breathe. Ooh, my face is burning."

She fanned herself with a pale blue paper napkin. "You play to win, don't you? You're not gonna let me catch my breath or think straight again any time soon, are you?"

He laughed, and though he wanted to touch her, he kept his hands to himself. Patience,

Hannibal believed, would be the key to his success with Josephine. "I can wait," he assured her. "I can wait. But first, there's one thing I've gotta do."

"What?"

"This."

What happened next was better than déjà vu for Josephine. The banked fires in Hannibal's around-the-world eyes blew high. He had her in his arms before she could blink twice.

In one fell swoop, he placed his mouth hard over her mouth in a brand that was utterly masculine and solely Hannibal Ray's. Pressed close against his body, she felt his every strong muscle, his every controlled desire. She wanted to rip his clothes off.

This time it was Hannibal who pulled away. "Not this way, baby. I want it all. The ring. The babies. Everything."

She wanted to shake him. "We can't stop now."

He looked grim, determined. "A month ago, I'd have agreed with you. Maybe even an hour ago, I'd have agreed with you, but now that the time is here, I know it's got to be all or nothing, Josephine. You decide."

Josephine felt like her pants were on fire and he wanted her to decide what she wanted to do about the rest of her life.

All . . . or . . . nothing.

Frustrated, she shoved his chest. "I can't make a decision like that when I feel so, uh, when I want to, uh . . ." She shoved him again. "Why are you spoiling everything! We were getting along so good!"

He grabbed both her wrists, but was careful not to hurt her. "For now, Josephine. We could go at it in every room in this house, but that won't change the fact that you won't leave the front yard. You won't even tell me you want me to stay after the repairs are done. I don't want a quick encounter. I want—" He stopped cold. He scratched his head. Finally, he laughed.

"What's so funny?"

"I don't have two beans to rub together and I'm hollering about a relationship. Who wants a bum? I'm crazy to think you would give up all this"—he swept his right arm wide—"to be my wife. I wouldn't be bringing anything to your table. I've never cared about material things, Josephine, and I guess I should have cared. It never mattered until now."

He walked to the door.

"Don't."

He stopped walking, but kept his back to her. "Don't leave the kitchen? Don't leave the farm? Don't leave Destiny? Don't what, Josephine?"

"Hannibal . . . I . . . why can't we be friends?"

He faced her then. "I don't want to be friends with you, Josephine. I want your body and your children and to grow old with you as husband and wife. Just friends doesn't cut it for me."

When he put it like that, it was not enough for her either. Josephine let him go, her heart on empty, her soul stripped bare. If only she could leave the front yard everything would be all right.

If . . . only . . . she had the courage to be strong.

THIRTEEN

The Brennon Farmhouse
Late February

Repairing the roof to the hundred-year-old farmhouse was easier said than done. Josephine's chickens were curious. Instead of running away from the sound of Hannibal's hammer, the chickens she kept as pets came to watch him work, most of them crowding around the base of the wooden ladder.

Using a mallet, he pounded a chisel along the grain of the shingles he needed to replace, until he had a series of strips. Working each strip loose slowly, he wiggled them until they broke free of the rusted nails holding them in place. To remove the nails, he cut them with the tip of a hacksaw, his hands protected with heavy leather gloves.

A new shingle was put into position, its butt running next to the old one. Roofing nails held the shingles down, and when he was done, Hannibal felt good. After he was gone from Destiny, he would be satisfied that neither wind nor rain would come through the roof of Josephine Brennon's house.

From his perch on the roof, Hannibal watched the Food on Wheels minivan pull in front of Josephine's white picket fence. The van parked almost exactly where the reverend's car had been weeks before. Within minutes, the van was loaded with Josephine's food.

As was her custom, she walked her company from the front door to the gate and not beyond the gate when it was time for her guest to leave her. She never went anywhere. She owned no transportation. She refused to leave the yard. The fluttering of Hannibal's heart came to him again, for longer this time, deeper this time, and the knowledge frightened him.

It frightened him because winter would soon be over and he felt responsible for Josephine. In good conscience, he could not leave Destiny in peace knowing she was unprotected.

Knowing she was unprotected tied in heavily with his sense of chivalry; good men protected children. Josephine was not a child in a legal way, but she had a child's way of seeing the world, a way of viewing things that both alarmed and charmed him. Except for the scar on her face, she lived the life of an innocent.

Innocent children trusted grown men on instinct. They relied on those subtle nonverbal cues that spoke of kindness and gentleness. It was for this reason, he felt, that when children were left to their own choosing, they often made choices based on what felt right.

What felt right.

Hannibal put away the ladder and tools, a deep aura of calm wrapping him tight within its circle of healing energy. All the extra thinking he had been doing since arriving in Destiny had come to a head.

It coupled with his instant need to protect and defend Josephine; to create a total lack of desire, to travel one step further. He was flooded with a profound peace he had not known since the first pickled peaches he tasted in his grandmother's tiny kitchen.

Hannibal had always wondered why, of all his mother's children, he had been born the restless one, the child never quite able to settle in one place for long.

Until now.

Decisive, Hannibal made his way to the cottage that was his new home. In the tiny bathroom, decorated with water schemes of blue and green, he showered away the dirt of a busy morning spent putting Josephine's land and his own life in order.

The work had served a higher purpose than the obvious one of making repairs. The automatic, repetitive work had allowed his mind long stretches of unbroken, deep, and free thought.

Stepping outside the cottage door onto the

brick walk lined with fragrant peppermint, Hannibal stomped the red dust off his single pair of cowboy boots.

He was going after a rose so one-of-a-kind that it defied logic or description. He was going after Josephine, a child raised in the winter of human neglect into a woman so rare, she changed the way he viewed himself in the world.

He had no desire to be a drifter anymore. He wanted to set roots. He no longer cared where he set them, as long as he could set them with Josephine. If it meant never leaving Destiny, then so be it.

Bare-headed, Hannibal made his way to Josephine's back door. He planned to skin her proverbial stem of thorns, one by one, until he reached the pinnacle of her beauty, the woman herself.

Josephine's nerves scattered with excitement at Hannibal's knock on her door. "It's open!"

"You look good, Josephine."

His voice rumbled through her chest like thunder. "I, uh, thank you." She motioned to a chair at the kitchen table. "Have a seat."

He did. "I see you're writing a grocery list."

"Yeah."

He had been around long enough to understand her method of operation when it came to business. "Who are you bartering with today to do your shopping?"

"Ivy Didwiddee."

He chuckled over the last name. "Poor woman."

"Don't be sorry for Ivy. She's so tough she makes Aunt Cordelia look like a cream puff."

He laughed out right. "Hard to imagine."

"Wait 'til you see her. Ivy is famous in Destiny for ruling the roost with an iron hand without raising her voice. She's no bigger than a minute, speaks soft enough for you to have to ask her to repeat what she said, and makes the best sweet potato pie you'll find between here and Texas."

"That good, huh?"

"The best."

"Coming from you, that's a real compliment."

"It's what Ivy says too. By the way, we're only having sandwiches for supper tonight."

"I'm glad."

"Why?"

"Besides the fact that I feel spoiled, you deserve the rest."

"Cooking is a huge outlet for me. I guess that's why I love it. But every now and then, I just want something easy to make. I hope you don't mind."

"Not at all. If it wasn't for you, I'd be eating fast food or a can of ravioli."

She looked him over. "You're too lean to be a fast-food junkie."

He was pleased she noticed he kept in shape. "One of the great things about working in small towns is that a lot of food is still made from scratch. There aren't Burger Kings or Taco Bells on every other corner."

She laughed, glad she read the daily newspaper. "We've got five fast-food chains in Destiny. All in the last five years too."

"Small towns tend to hang on to their smallness by keeping chain stores to a minimum."

"True, but it also serves a larger purpose."

"Which is?"

"Small business ownership. In a small town like Destiny, my small business is actually big business. I really feel as if what I do matters," she said, pride reflected in her voice.

He nodded once in agreement. "When I have steady work, I find a good mom-and-pop family restaurant and wear it out until my job is done."

"Smart."

"Almost as smart as you."

"What do you mean?"

"You haven't told me what you do for Ivy."

Josephine fiddled with the red band at her hair, a nervous gesture Hannibal now recognized. He said, "You don't have to tell me anything. I was just curious."

"It's not that . . . it's just that, well, not too many people know about my arrangement with Ivy."

"They have to know she's shopping for you."

"Yeah, but they have no idea I teach her to read."

Hannibal doubted much else about Josephine's friends or enemies could surprise him, but he was wrong. "You're kidding."

"No. A lot of people, old and young, skip out of school at an early age to run farms or just plain run out of town."

"What's her story?"

"It's hard to believe, but her mother died in a cotton field from exhaustion and heat stroke back in 1975."

It took little imagination for Hannibal to figure out the rest. "So, Ivy took on the raising of her siblings?"

"Right."

"Was her father around?"

"Sure. He was a janitor by night and a field worker by day. Ivy had plenty of help from family and neighbors, but as the oldest of six, she really got the short end of the stick. Her four sisters went on to college."

"Why didn't Ivy go back to school?"

"Pride. She ended up owning the janitorial service where her daddy worked until he got too rickety from arthritis. He's still alive and she takes care of him. Together they've built up the business. Ivy's daddy helped me start up mine."

Hannibal realized that Josephine was not alone after all. People cared about her and helped her out in ways that made her comfortable. "Did he come here?"

"No. He actually worked it through Aunt Cordelia, of all people. She was taking my cakes and pies and what not to so many church functions, people kept asking when she found time to be in the kitchen so much."

"And she confessed she wasn't the cook?"

"I didn't believe it either. Anyway, Ivy's daddy, Mr. Didwiddee, found out and . . . well, knowing how I like to . . . stick around the house, he suggested I start a business where I sell my food to the churches."

"Makes sense."

"Yeah, but a lot of folks were against it."

"Don't tell me. I can guess."

"Go on."

"I imagine they said something like food for the needy should be given cash-free and from the kindness of the donor's heart."

She smiled. "Pretty much. Truth is, feeding people by the hundreds is expensive, and it's tiring for the volunteers. Aunt Cordelia's church, The Good Faith Baptist Church, started things off. I pretty much sell to them exclusively, although I have made food for charity fund-raisers sponsored by neighboring churches."

"Aunt Cordelia's handiwork?"

"Yeah. Even though she doesn't do any of the cooking, she shares some of the limelight because I'm her niece. Mostly, people are impressed I'm able to survive the way I do without actually leaving my land. To be honest, I'm a charity case."

"Because of your face."

"Yeah."

"I think it's more than that, Josephine. I think it's a collective guilt."

He was pissing her off. "Are you saying I couldn't be a success without this town's support?"

"Yes and no."

"You think I'm not strong enough to make it on my own?"

"Yes and no."

"Don't get cagey on me, Hannibal."

He broke his meaning down for her. "More than likely, you'd have been raised in child protective custody had you lived in a big city. In Destiny, it sounds to me as if you were pretty much raised with the village concept. Had you grown up in the foster care system, you probably would not have had resources like the Didwiddees to rely on for stability. Anybody can start a business, Josephine, but it takes a stable person to grow a business into a profitable venture."

She settled down again. "You've got a point."

"I also see that even though your Aunt Cordelia is rude to you, she's actually an anchor."

She blew him off with a wave of her hand. "Give me a break."

"She checks on you constantly. So does the reverend and those two ladies he totes around with him."

"Aunt Cordelia and her friends don't give a hoot about me."

"I disagree. You have a house to live in that you inherited. You do have friends, just not people your own age. Didn't you go to school, Josephine?"

She stood up. "I'm tired."

He pulled her back down. "It's two o'clock in the afternoon. Didn't you go to school?"

"Of course."

"Did you finish?"

She looked away. "I've got to call Ivy so I can tell her this grocery list is ready."

"When did you drop out?"

She smoothed a palm down her hair. Once. Twice.

"Was it before or after your face was burned with that stupid cattle iron?"

"After." Her glare was nothing nice.

Neither was the tone of his voice. "Who burned you, Josephine?"

"I'm not telling."

"Was it Cordelia?"

"Leave me alone."

"Was it the reverend?"

"Stop."

Frustrated, he felt like shaking her out of her boots. "Who did it, Josephine?"

"I don't think about that anymore. I don't

want to think about it anymore. You've got no
right to ask me to think about it now."

He stared at her with fierce concentration.
He saw no reason to beat around the bush.
Everything about his relationship with Jose-
phine was too intense for subtle conversation.
"I still want you."

"You can't have me."

His manner was laid-back, but the power of
his words came on strong. "But I will."

She was a rebel with a cause and the cause
was her own self-preservation. "Just because I
live alone doesn't mean I'm starving for a
man. I'm sure there are a lot of single women
in the world who have less going on for them
than I do."

"You're right," he conceded. "You've got
land. Your own home. A thriving business.
Maybe you don't need somebody to love, but
I do, Josephine."

Sheer thrill raced through her. "Me?"

"You."

He was so smooth, but she was no easy pick-
ings. "I think you'd better take your sandwich
and go."

"I'll take my sandwich but I'll go when I'm
good and damned ready."

In the privacy of her mind, Josephine ac-
knowledged how much she enjoyed their spar-
ring match. "Squatter's rights?"

"I'm a friend, Josephine."

"Friends don't throw their weight around."

"Friends who want to be more than friends do. You've got more thorns on you than those roses on your front porch, but one of these days, you'll be mine, Josephine."

Blood roared through her ears. "Why?"

She was a fighter with the soul of a wounded child. "Why you?"

"Yeah."

"I admire you for being able to live in solitude the way you do. I am awed that in spite of your quiet lifestyle, you are not out of shape or without spirit. You've got moxie, Josephine. I respect that."

She wanted to believe him. She really did. "None of which explains why you'd be interested in me as a woman. I'm as ugly as that red dirt you're always stomping off your boots."

"That dirt is as old and symbolic of the South as honeysuckle vine. Nothing like that can be ugly. Strength in a woman can't be ugly, not when it's tempered with sweetness the way it is in you."

"You're saying you'd be . . . comfortable taking me out in public?"

"Yes."

She never trusted anyone completely, ever. Did she dare believe him? "Liar."

He swiped his hand over his face. "Don't start that up again." She was complex—tough, fragile, hard, soft, defiant, needy. She spoiled his taste for any other woman.

"People would stare," she continued. "They always stare. Kids point or they laugh. I hate that."

"You have every right to hate it. You also have to be sensible enough to understand that kind of curiosity."

"I got tired of being sensible, which is really about turning the other cheek. I've only got one good one. When it comes to generosity, I used that last cheek all up."

"What grade did you get tired of trying?"

"Seventh grade."

"You have a sixth-grade education, yet you teach Ivy Didwiddee how to read in exchange for shopping privileges."

"Yeah."

Her revelation increased his attraction to her. "That's incredible."

"Don't make fun of me."

He locked fingers with hers. "Ivy's father taught you business management?"

"Ivy did. Her father kept telling me I could do it."

"And you did."

"Yeah."

"I'm proud of you."

She studied the rough, calloused hand and marveled at how seamlessly he had merged with her life. "I don't know what to say."

Her admission unraveled a silken coil in his heart. "Say you'll marry me. I'm a really nice guy."

"Yeah. You're a really nice guy who can't stay put from one season to the next."

"I would stay here."

"Get real."

He gazed into her lovely, belligerent face and wondered about all the pieces in the puzzle of his life that had clicked him forward to this place in time. It was as if the edges of the puzzle of his life had been snapped together first, slowly moving toward the center of his destiny, toward Josephine. "You could come with me."

"I haven't been anywhere except to the old pole shed, and you tore that down yesterday."

He glanced at her mouth. "We can make this work."

Josephine's heart fluttered an instant. She decided that he wore brute power like a second skin. Hannibal's entire persona was as unnerving to her as it was starkly intimate.

He acted as if he had no other place to be than by her side. She repressed a thrill of flat-out lust. "The man who gets me won't be a rambling man, Hannibal Ray. It won't be a man with one pair of boots, a worn-out Stetson, a sheepskin coat, three pairs of jeans, five shirts and a box full of essentials."

His know-everything eyes were naked with sensuality. "Been paying attention, have you?"

His laugh was low, male, and black as the night was long. She enjoyed the sound of it, even while her body shivered.

Desire shone like fire from the gold hues within her eyes even as she gathered all her bravado to stalk off in a huff. "Dinner is self-serve," she said over her shoulder.

He raised his voice over the stomping of her feet on the gleaming hardwood floor. "I'm not a quitter, Josephine."

"And I'm no piece of cake!"

"No," he spoke low to himself, "you're priceless."

FOURTEEN

Cordelia Brennon's Home
Early March

Cordelia Brennon busied herself inside her two-bedroom home, her mind fully intent on cleaning up even though her house appeared spotless already. It was a nervous habit.

No music interrupted her efficient work flow. The methodical process had been honed by many years of obsessive-compulsive behavior. Instead of the hum of an electrical charge, the only sound in the house she occupied alone was the sound of the Bissell vacuum cleaner sucking dirt off the carpet.

Clear thinking kept her goals in perfect sight. For Cordelia, success was achieved through the fine-tuning of details. She nodded a fraction in silent self-congratulation. She believed she was living proof that success was never someone else's will, or coincidence, or even an accident.

A frown of distaste marred her brow. Incorporating the stranger into the complex nature of her life with Josephine was a tricky thing. For a short moment, the Bissell stopped its greedy suction, then resumed its course across the carpet.

She was a practical woman and practical women used logic to move through life, not vague feelings of unease. She chalked the foreboding to Josephine's uncharacteristic display of affection; she absolutely beamed in the presence of the stranger. Cordelia's frown deepened.

It had not been an easy task to separate herself from the pain of the past, but she had, step by step, detail by detail, until her mission had been accomplished. Until the stranger's arrival, there had been few struggles for power between herself and Josephine.

Yes, she mused, her right index finger clicking the red switch on the Bissell to OFF, the stranger had definitely changed things between the Brennon women.

Cordelia put the Bissell in the coat closet near the tiny foyer, her movements unhurried, her lips pushed into a crocodile's smile as she considered how ill-equipped Josephine was to deal with Hannibal Ray. Soon, she would realize she was in way over her head; soon, she would send him packing.

Cordelia removed an ostrich feather duster from the top shelf of the coat closet where she stored the vacuum cleaner. With studious care, she put the genuine feathers to work over the dark mahogany tables in the living room. The monotonous work calmed her. Her frown disappeared.

The drifter had singled out Josephine as a woman in need of protection. Why? Cordelia returned the ostrich feather duster to the shelf in the closet. The reverend was right. Something about the drifter smelled distinctly of trouble.

Cordelia glanced around her tiny bungalow. Filled with mahogany furniture, it was surprisingly devoid of personal paraphernalia. There were no family photographs, no lifetime collection of knickknacks.

Her place was hotel-room functional: basic furniture, with appropriate lamps, and tasteful, contemporary wall art. The color scheme was monochromatic in shades ranging from light pink to mauve to nearly purple.

The television and radio were turned off as she paced around the house wishing she had something constructive to do. She looked out the living room window.

There were thick clouds packed tight together. A storm was coming. She could feel it in her shoulder bones. She dialed Shirley Louise.

"Hello?"

"What's up, Shirley Louise?"

"Storm's coming."

"Your back aching?"

"Hands and ankles too. Doc Billings says it's an old wives' tale that people with arthritis can feel storms coming on long before they hit."

"Doc Billings is like the rest of the quacks practicing medicine. They need science to prove to 'em what folks been saying since they could talk."

"I guess that's why they use the word *practice.*"

"Never thought about it, but you're right."

"What's really on your mind, Cordelia?"

"Just shootin' the breeze."

"We go back to first grade, Cordelia. You don't shoot the breeze."

"You're telling me a friend can't call a friend just because?"

"Whenever it storms you call me. Fact is, I don't even try to hit the sack anymore until we've had our little wet-weather chat."

"Shoot, Shirley Louise. Am I really that predictable?"

"About some things, you are. I guess that's true about most of us."

"I didn't know my calling you like this was a problem."

"It might be a problem if you called me every time it rained, but you don't. You only call me when there's severe weather."

Cordelia chuckled. "Sometimes we talk so long on the phone, I've often wondered why we didn't get struck by lightning."

"You're worried about Josephine too."

"She's just like Marvella."

"No, she isn't," Shirley Louise countered.

"She looks just like her."

"She may look like Marvella, but she acts like you."

"Please."

"I'm serious, Cordelia. You both are stubborn. I think Josephine didn't go back to school as much out of spite against you as any other reason."

"Her face—"

"It's old hat at this point. The young generation in Destiny knows her by legend only."

"Legend my foot. People think she's crazy the way she lives in that house by herself."

"Crazy or not, Cordelia, people respect her. Kids come to her place on Halloween as easy as the next house. If she was crazy, her place would be considered a haunted house or something. It would get teepeed with toilet paper or slammed with raw eggs. Kids don't do that to her because whatever they hear about Josephine is largely good."

"They throw crap at my house."

"And you cuss 'em out for doing it too. Cordelia, you've got a real reputation for talking first and thinking later."

"That ain't it and you know it. People hate me because they think I'm the reason Josephine is all messed up."

"Except for the scar on her face, Josephine is just fine. You're the one that's messed up."

"Don't go there, Shirley Louise. I've got a social life."

"You don't have a life at all."

"I got church. I got friends at work too."

"You're a clerk in the county courthouse and you've been a clerk in the county courthouse for twenty-one years. You go to work. Go to church. You go home. When you get bored you try to tick Josephine off. Matter of fact, I'm the one with a screw loose because I let you push me into bugging Josephine just to make you happy. She's more mature than you, me, Bea, and Reverend Franklin too."

"What's got into you tonight, Shirley Louise? Why are you being so . . . so—"

"Honest?"

"Catty is more like it."

"Want the truth?"

"Ain't that what you been doing all night, Shirley Louise? Telling the truth the way you see it?"

"Seeing Josephine with that handsome handyman of hers got me to thinking about how petty we all are. I mean, Josephine has a meaningful life. She doesn't work for the county like you do and she doesn't work at dispatch in the emergency room like I do. She's at home making money doing something she's gonna do whether she gets paid for it or not. She's living the American dream, Cordelia Brennon. We're two miserable old spinsters."

"I'm not miserable."

"Stuff it, Cordelia. You're in love with a man who won't be seen with you in public. What woman in her right mind could be happy with that?"

"What man?"

"Don't get me started. You know full well I'm talking about the reverend."

"Me and him are just friends."

"In a pig's eye. You love him. He don't love you."

Cordelia stopped faking it. "He wanted Marvella. All the men wanted Marvella."

"And you hated your sister because of it, didn't you? You hated her because she ran off with that piano player when you wanted him yourself."

"She stole him."

"You never had him in the first place, Cordelia."

"I did too."

"He was Freda's cousin from the sticks. He could not dance worth a lick but he played that piano like nobody's business. You just plain threw yourself at him, Cordelia. Marvella was the one in the shadow."

"No, she wasn't."

"She wasn't pushy, and matter of fact, she wore brown most of the time just like Josephine. Funny, I hadn't really thought about that until now."

"Marvella was a slut."

"She didn't sleep around, Cordelia. You did."

"I don't know why I'm talking to you anyway."

"Besides the reverend, I'm about the only person you can talk to. That's why you didn't jump down my throat when I told you I know you and him are a couple. I can't believe two middle-aged people think they can sneak around town for twenty years and keep it a secret. Ain't nothing secret going on in Destiny."

"That handyman."

"Where did he come from?"

"Don't know."

"Josephine didn't tell you?"

"I guess I never asked."

"A storm is ready to bust open any minute. She's in the house alone with a man don't a soul in Destiny know a thing about. She hates storms more than you do. Why is that, Cordelia? What is it about storms that tears you and Josephine up?"

"Nothing."

"Tell me. After all these years, I deserve to know."

"Let's get back to that part about Josephine being in the house with a man by herself. He lives out back."

"Says who?"

"Says Josephine."

"Wake up, sister. I saw the way he looked at

her. Josephine is young and beautiful in a tragic, gothic novel kind of way."

"All right, you Phyllis Whitney wanna-be."

"I'm serious, Cordelia. Don't you think it's romantic to have this big, dashing stranger come in from the cold to be Josephine's hero?"

"He's only been here a short while."

"A short while of concentrated time with a woman who must blow his mind every day. Josephine is extremely intelligent. She is devoted to that stupid house. She is young. She wants to be loved just like you and just like me. Only she's got more guts than the two of us put together. She went out and grabbed herself a man."

"Ain't that exactly what I said? She's just like my sister. Marvella went out and grabbed herself a man too. A stranger."

"Cordelia, everything done in this world is done for a reason. Marvella did what she had to do with a man nobody saw before or after he left Destiny. If it wasn't for that man, Josephine wouldn't be here."

"Got that straight. She was a mistake."

Shirley Louise put her foot down. She drew a line in their relationship. "No."

"She was."

"If Josephine wasn't here, you'd be all alone, Cordelia. You'd have to choke on your guilt instead of being able to fight it by fighting Josephine."

"Didn't know you was a head doctor."

"I should have spoken my mind years ago. I keep going to church hoping I can cleanse my spirit of being your . . . your partner in crime. I'm as bad as you are for letting you tear into Josephine the way I do. I should have walked away from you like most everybody else in town that ain't from the bottom of the barrel."

"What are you saying, Shirley Louise?"

"I'm saying it's your fault Marvella is dead. I'm saying that in some twisted kind of way, you've aided and abetted Josephine into being a . . . a hermit because you wanted to protect her."

"From what?"

"From herself. I think you've got her so twisted up with Marvella that you can't see her for the woman she really is. I think you had me and Bea and the reverend go visit Josephine because you needed some moral support for yourself."

"And you think I'm crazy? You're the one that don't make no sense."

"If I was so crazy you wouldn't be calling me up to stabilize you every time the sky cracks open. You think it's hell breaking loose when tornado weather comes. Don't you?"

Cordelia paused a long time. "I can't even come close to figuring you out tonight, Shirley Louise."

"You need moral support because all your

hard work at keeping Josephine from turning out like Marvella backfired. She met a stranger from nowhere and he's so fine you're scared he's gonna take her away. If he took her away, you'd finally have to look in the mirror, Cordelia. If I was you I couldn't do that. Not with a soul as black as yours."

"Why are you being so cruel?" It was a whisper.

"I hate myself for not standing up for Josephine. I hate myself for being a coward when that little girl needed a friend."

"You're my friend."

"I'm your crutch."

"No."

"Yes. When you let Josephine drop out of junior high I should never have talked Bea into getting that girl home-school papers. When Josephine did just enough work to pass, and then stopped altogether, it was Bea who pulled strings and let Josephine fall by the wayside. Bea is guilty. I'm guilty. You're guilty. What's the reverend guilty about, Cordelia? How did he do Josephine wrong?"

"Be quiet."

Shirley Louise would not be quiet. She was a freight train of truth. "We're all living miserable lives because we're cowards. You could have left Destiny and found a musician if you'd really wanted one. You could have done anything. You didn't. You stayed and got bitter."

"If I hadn't stayed, I wouldn't have been able to take on Josephine."

"I don't see how you did her any favors."

"I left her that house."

"Marvella left her that house. You rent that cracker box you call home. The only thing that surprises me is that Josephine keeps that place looking fabulous but she won't fix that broken window on the second floor. Why is that, Cordelia?"

"Ask her."

"I'm asking you."

"Well, you're asking the wrong person."

"Okay, why is it that if you packed up your suitcase and a box of junk, your house would look empty?"

"I don't know what you mean."

"Of course you do. Josephine's got a house so fine, people feel honored when they get inside. Her yard is so spectacular, she's got some kind of flower in bloom year round. She's got roses in December and come January, while there is still snow on the ground, she'll have crocus coming up out around that big old cottonwood in her front yard."

"Her house ought to be nice since she don't leave it."

"No," Shirley Louise admitted. "She doesn't get out into the world, but she managed to bring the world to her. You could go anywhere but you don't. Unlike Josephine, you rarely have company. Your house is nice, but it isn't friendly. It don't welcome people the way Josephine's place does. You've had a man all these years but it ain't done you a bit of good. Josephine's got a man and her little face is beaming. I hope he sweeps her off her feet. I hope he takes her away from here."

"She can't leave."

"Why not?"

"She has to feed the homeless and old crazy folks like you."

"The homeless will get fed regardless. So will the elderly. Josephine just makes it easy on Good Faith Baptist Church. Most of the women who'd be doing all the cooking she does have families and jobs and meetings and whatever. They don't have time to do what she does. It's a beneficial arrangement. The food is uniform. It tastes good. And the women of Good Faith can free their conscience about not standing up for Josephine. You're the one who should have been cast out from the flock, Cordelia. Not Josephine."

"She could go to church!"

"The same people she wanted to avoid in school are the same people who walk around Destiny every day, the same people who go to the churches in Destiny. Like I said, Josephine is a lot like you when it comes to the stubborn department."

"You mean she's trying to spite me."

"You and a whole lot of other people, Cordelia. You, me, Bea, and the reverend are just the tip of the old iceberg. She's living in a paradise and we're living in a hell of our own making. Nothing you can do will ever be right until you come out with the truth about Marvella dying. You have to admit what you done to her. It's the only way to repent."

"What about you, Miss Suddenly Righteous?"

"I've got to put you down."

"What?"

"We can't be friends no more, Cordelia. It just ain't right."

Cordelia slammed the phone down. First the reverend, then Shirley Louise. It was Josephine's fault. Storm or no storm, tonight she was going to pay.

FIFTEEN

The Brennon Farmhouse
The Same Night

Josephine was not afraid of the coming storm. She sat alone in her living room, a single lamp on for light. Her wits were sharp, her body alive with anticipation. Cordelia always came to her in a storm, either over the phone or in person.

Always.

In the wake of Marvella's death, there had been no forgiveness between the two remaining Brennon women. Josephine understood she could never hope to live a normal life with Hannibal as long as she was haunted by her mother's shadow, a shadow that haunted Cordelia as well.

And so it was that in the deep stillness of her living room, Josephine gathered close the full power of her oneness, a strength honed by the many years she had lived with no one.

Outside the living room, thunder boomed

loud enough to make dishes rattle in the china hutch. The floor vibrated. Josephine saw lightning strike.

The wind cut through the bare limbs of sycamores and willows and cottonwoods until it kicked up enough speed to scream. The wind careened around the farmhouse, over the roof and along the eaves.

It threw tiny debris against the windows. Soon it would rain. Even though she was tempted to invite Hannibal to stay with her, Josephine made no move to summon him; this was a fight she needed to battle on her own.

A banging on the front door made her jump. She opened the door quickly. "Come in, Cordelia."

The older woman kicked the door shut with the heel of one basic black boot. "Not aunt. Just Cordelia, huh?" Her tone was sly.

Josephine motioned for her guest to sit down. "Let's get this over with. I don't really want to argue with you, but since we haven't had a civil conversation in God knows how long, I don't expect we'll have one tonight either."

Cordelia leaned against the door, her short gray-brown hair whipped by the wind. "I don't expect we'll have one either and it ain't because we don't play nice. It's the storm. It was storming the night you showed up in Destiny."

Looking at her aunt's small, vicious eyes, Josephine knew that if she remained a recluse,

she would wind up as miserable and alone as
Cordelia. Despite her animosity, Josephine reminded herself that Cordelia was her mother's
sister and deserved kindness for this reason.
"I have cold tea if you want some."

Cordelia finally sat down. "Water. All of a
sudden my throat is so dry I can't hardly swal-
low."

Josephine came back with the water, which
she sat on the coffee table. "What's on your
mind?"

"Hannibal Ray."

Like Cordelia, Josephine preferred to get
straight to the point. "I didn't think you remembered his name."

"I remember a lot of things. Where is he
at?"

"His place."

Cordelia picked up the glass of water, then
set it down again without a taste. "I kind of
thought he'd be here with you."

"He works for me, Cordelia. He doesn't live
with me. He lives in the cottage."

Cordelia tossed her pocketbook on an armchair. "Why did you hire him?"

"We've been over this before. The farm
needs fixing up."

Cordelia slammed her palm on the coffee
table. "It's more than that and you know it."

"Grown women do what they want to do.
I'm grown."

"You're trying to spite me, aren't you?"

Josephine leaned forward, her voice hard. "It's a little late for that, don't you think?"

"It's never too late for revenge."

"What's your point?"

Cordelia had come to Josephine's to raise hell, but when she thought about everything Shirley Louise said on the phone, she felt . . . ashamed. Maybe it really was time for some truth. "You want to hurt me. Pay me back."

The truth was unexpected, but well-received. It was the beginning of justice for Josephine. She said, "We can't change the past."

Cordelia was quick to reply. "But we can make others suffer for it." They both knew she referred to herself.

Josephine snorted. "I'm the one who has suffered the most. You're the one walking around Destiny free to do whatever you want to do. Nobody points fingers when you come around."

"You're wrong. People stare at me all the time because they blame me for the way you live. I'm only tolerated around town. If you came out of this house sometime, you would know it."

Josephine jumped to her feet. "I don't care how you're treated. I don't care about you at all." She did care, though. Good or bad, Cordelia had been a constant in her life.

Cordelia jumped to her feet too. "How can you say that, Josephine? I'm your blood kin."

Josephine had no stomach for a hypocrite.

"You treat me like crap because you're ashamed about everything you haven't done."

"You live better than I do."

"So?"

"People respect you."

"So?"

"I'm tired of being blamed for something I didn't do. Marvella is the cause of all our troubles."

Now they were getting somewhere. "You kicked my mother to the curb when she needed you the most. I thought you came here to talk about the truth."

"She stole my man." Cordelia hissed the words. Even after all these years, the wound of Marvella's betrayal remained fresh.

"How could she steal what you never had?"

Cordelia's anger was its own driving force. She prowled the living room, touching nothing, seeing nothing. "There's things about Marvella you don't know, Josephine. She only seems nicer than me because she's dead. People always think better of the dead than they do of the living."

Josephine shook her head in disbelief. "If you want sympathy, Cordelia, you've come to the wrong person."

"Stud Bishop was mine, I tell you. We . . . before he left town with Marvella, he . . . we, uh, we spent some time together."

"You had sex with him?"

"Yes."

"Why bring that up now? Mama can't deny it and it doesn't matter anyway."

Cordelia stopped pacing to stand before the empty fireplace. "It matters a lot."

"Why?"

"Marvella ran off with Stud. Didn't you ever wonder why your mama didn't call you by his last name?"

"Some women keep their own name as a matter of pride."

"Not Marvella. You think she was a saint, but she was worse than I am."

"That's impossible."

"You're a Brennon." Cordelia met Josephine's belligerent gaze. "I'm a Brennon."

"So?"

Cordelia faltered. The Brennon family had not been bound by love. Instead, they had been bound by sorrow and pain. The cycle was pitiful and could only be stopped with the truth. "I'm . . . I'm . . . she didn't . . . you aren't . . ."

Josephine had never seen Cordelia so out of sorts. It alarmed her. "Whatever you're trying to say, just say it."

"Marvella was not your mother." There. She had said it. Cordelia's chin tilted up a notch.

Josephine's laughter was a bitter, ugly thing in the too-dark living room. "You raised me, Cordelia, but you didn't want to. You tolerated me but you were never my mother."

"I am your mother, Josephine."

"No! You told me over and over again that Mama died because she didn't take good care of herself. You said if she had taken care of herself the right way, I never would have been homeless!"

Even Cordelia was appalled by the reality of those hateful words thrown at a young, innocent child. Her cruelty had been extreme, and it was probably too late to make a difference. Still, she had to try. "Marvella also died of a broken heart, Josephine. I ought to know because I'm the one who did the breaking."

"You aren't making sense."

Cordelia grabbed Josephine's hands. She squeezed hard enough to hurt her. "Me and your mama shared the same man, but she didn't know what I was doing."

Josephine yanked her hands away. "That's sick."

"Maybe, but I loved your daddy. Stud Bishop was every bit as handsome to me as Hannibal Ray is to you."

"It's different. I'm not in love with Hannibal."

"I think you are."

"I barely know him."

"Maybe not with your mind, but I believe you know him with your heart. Marvella wanted Stud Bishop with her mind. She saw him as an easy way to get out of Destiny. I wanted Stud Bishop with my heart."

"What did Stud Bishop want?"

"A good time. He liked women. Trouble is, he wasn't careful about his selection. His women had to be pretty and convenient and willing to let him do his own thing. He liked to party. Playing the piano opened doors to lots of parties." Cordelia clasped her hands tightly together. "Our lives are full of doors, Josephine. Front doors. Back doors. Doors to opportunity."

"You're talking riddles."

"Stud walked through front doors when he wanted people to know what he was up to. He came through back doors when he didn't. He came through the front door of our house, this house, to court me but he came through the back door to court your mama."

"She got pregnant."

"No, Josephine. I'm the one who got pregnant."

"What?"

Cordelia' s voice trembled. "You really are my daughter."

"What in the world?"

"Marvella stole you and ran off with Stud Bishop before the cord dried on your navel. I was all stoved up in bed, hurting and supposedly resting while she took care of you one day. When I woke up, all three of you were gone."

Josephine had to sit down. "But . . ."

"Your mama ran off to Texas and she stayed in Texas until she came crawling home with syphilis, of all things." Cordelia said the word *syphilis* as if she was still surprised.

Josephine kept shaking her head. "I can't believe what you're saying!" It meant Shirley Louise, Bea, the reverend, and the rest of the old-timers in Destiny had to know the truth about Josephine's beginnings. "I don't believe you."

"Believe it. Stud was a philanderer. He never married your mother. She caught syphilis from him and was too stupid to get help. By the time she came home to me in Destiny, it was already too late." Cordelia's tone gave the impression she felt Marvella got what she deserved for stealing Josephine and her piano-playing father.

"Why did she come back?"

"She came back to make things right between us. She came back to give me my little girl."

Josephine almost laughed at the irony. She, a recluse, was in the middle of a talk show–style drama. She could hardly believe the treachery of the blood sisters. Shirley Louise and Bea were more kind to each other than Marvella and Cordelia had been.

"Where's my father?" Josephine demanded.

"Living somewhere in Texas I guess. The bastard got help for himself, but Marvella had too much pride to go to a doctor. She kept trying home cures and when that didn't help, she came back to Destiny. Reverend Franklin prayed over her, but that didn't save her either. Me, Shirley Louise, and Bea all prayed for Marvella, but it was way too late to save her. Basically, she came back to Destiny to die and make sure you had a future."

Bitterness ran through Josephine like blood. Now she knew why the reverend and his Christian sisters were Cordelia's partners in crime; they knew the truth about Marvella's death and Josephine's birth. Even knowing the truth, they had aided and abetted Cordelia's need for revenge.

"Why did you lie to me all these years?"

"Your mama believed that taking Stud Bishop's baby would make him want her. He thought she was crazy and he really didn't care. He figured what me and Marvella did between us about you was me and Marvella's business. He wasn't into raising babies, just making babies. Some men are like that, Josephine. They define their manhood by the number of living children they can count. Stud Bishop was like that."

"Which explains why he didn't take me in when Mama died." Josephine was glad to finally know why.

"Yes, it does."

Parts of her past had always been fuzzy. She had been living a life of half-truths and raised by a bunch of secret-keepers. "How old was I when you took me in?"

"Four."

"But all these years, you've acted like you

hated me. How could you hate your own flesh and blood?"

Cordelia sat on the sofa. "I didn't . . . I don't . . . hate you."

Josephine sat on an armchair. The coffee table was between them, Cordelia's water glass untouched. "What's wrong, then?"

"I hated Marvella. I hated her for taking you away from me. Every time I saw you I was reminded of her treachery."

"But it wasn't my fault."

Cordelia looked as if she had aged five years in five minutes. "No. It's usually the children who suffer for the mistakes of grown folks."

"You should have been happy to get me back." So much time had been wasted building walls of distrust and disharmony.

"I was and I wasn't happy. I was glad to know you were all right, but you . . . you didn't like me when you met me, Josephine."

"You've always been so distant and hateful, Aunt Cordelia."

"I was really mad at Marvella and I guess I took my anger out on you. I was ten years older than her, so I remember what she was like as a baby. She was like you. I didn't want you to turn out like her, so I did my best to make you different."

"You wouldn't let boys call me on the phone or stop by the house."

The lines around Cordelia's mouth grew tight. "That's right."

"The only girls I got to play with after school were the girls who went to Bible study at the different churches in Destiny. You took away my childhood, Aunt Cordelia."

"I didn't tell you to quit school."

"You didn't tell me to stay, either."

Cordelia shrugged. "It was a way to clean up the past. Out of sight, out of mind."

"I grew up wishing it was you that died and not my mama. I hated living with you."

"Is that why you ran off behind the chicken coop with Ivy Didwiddee's baby brother?"

"Me and Darnell weren't doing anything."

Cordelia scoffed. "He was holding your hand."

"We were twelve years old!"

"Marvella was sixteen when she stole you away from me."

"You ruined my life!"

"No, Josephine. You ruined your life."

Josephine slapped Cordelia so hard, the woman fell back on the couch.

Cordelia launched herself at Josephine. "Oh no, Marvella, you ain't gonna be the one doin' all the hittin' around here tonight."

"I AM NOT MARVELLA!"

The four words stopped Cordelia cold. "Dear God? What are we doing?"

Josephine was shaking with rage. "Ending things for good, Aunt Cordelia. Mother. Whoever you are. I don't want to see you again."

"I'm sorry, Josephine."

"It's too late to be sorry. You have picked and poked and scraped me raw with your comparisons of me to my mother. She was sixteen and living with a man a good ten years older than she was, Cordelia. You should have gone after her and brought her back. You should have brought me back."

"I tried to find you."

"Texas is only one state away. You couldn't have tried that hard."

"You're right. I didn't."

"Why?"

"I figured she had to come crawling back at some point to ask me for forgiveness. I didn't expect it to take four years and a deadly disease to do it. I think if Stud Bishop had been even halfway decent, she would have left him with you and I never would have seen you again."

"Why did you squander our happiness?"

"For the same reason your face is messed up."

A nerve beneath Josephine's eye twitched. "If only you had spoken the truth sooner."

Cordelia snorted in disgust. "What, Josephine? Things would be different? You're every bit as spiteful as I am."

"You made me this way."

"Which is why I'm here tonight."

It was too little too late. Josephine rebelled. "You don't want me to run off with Hannibal just to piss you off."

"You know me well. I'm afraid for you, Josephine. I'm afraid you'll do something reckless. All that brown doesn't fool me. It's the red band on your head that's the real you."

"Go home, Cordelia."

"I'm your mother."

"My mother is dead. You said so yourself."

Their relationship had hit its bottom. "You have every right to feel bitter."

"No kidding."

"But don't hurt yourself to spite me."

Cordelia's delayed concern infuriated Josephine. She pointed a thumb in the direction of the cottage. "Hannibal is a good man. He's not some old coot chasing young girls, like . . . like my father. Hannibal hasn't laid a hand on me."

"Maybe not yet. But I've seen the way your face lights up when he comes around. I've seen the way he protects you. Hannibal isn't at all like your daddy. I guess that's what really scares me, Josephine. He could take you away from here and I . . . I won't . . ."

"You won't get the chance to do the right thing by me. That's why you're here tonight. You want forgiveness."

"Yes."

Josephine's eyes turned to slits of rage. Her voice was cold. "You don't deserve it. I should turn you away the way you did my mother."

"Untreated venereal disease killed Marvella."

"If you hadn't been so angry with her, maybe she would have come back home before it was too late. Maybe she wouldn't have died."

"Don't you see, Josephine? Marvella couldn't come home. She had the same kind of pride that I have. That you have. Brennon women are stubborn women, but we're strong too."

"Don't."

"Don't what?"

"Don't try to . . . to make us sound like a unit . . . like we've got some kind of connection."

"We do have a connection. You are my daughter, Josephine. Marvella was my sister and I know she loved you enough for both of us. She didn't let you down. I let you down. You're right. I should have been glad to have you back. Instead of being glad you were back, I was hung up on the fact that you cried when I touched you and you didn't recognize me as your mother."

Josephine's voice relaxed. In truth, she felt sick at the time she could never regain with Cordelia. "I was a newborn when I left Destiny. It was impossible for me to know any better. Besides, at four, you could have trained me to call you mama. I probably would have called you mama on my own out of love if you had tried to make me feel welcome in your life. I grew up feeling like I was a burden. I had no father and no mother. My friends were so care-

fully scrutinized that my social life was limited
to the church scene."

"Is that why you don't go to church?"

"Reverend Franklin is why I don't go to
church. The man is a hypocrite and I figure
if he's a hypocrite then so are the rest of the
preachers in this town. It takes a conspiracy to
keep a secret like the one you've been keeping."

"You're wrong, Josephine. There are a lot
of good religious men in this town."

Josephine kicked the sofa. "I'm only talking
about one man, Aunt Cordelia. Your man. The
reverend."

"Don't be cruel."

"If I'm cruel, it's because you made me this
way."

"What about Hannibal?"

"He's my friend. You won't be scaring him
off forever the way you did Ivy Didwiddee's little brother. In case you haven't noticed, I'm
not a runner. If I was, I'd have been gone a
long time ago."

Cordelia asked the one question that no one
had the answer to except Josephine. "What
keeps you here, Josephine?" The words were
hushed, ripe with tension.

"This house."

SIXTEEN

At the same time the women argued, the storm struck Destiny with the force of a powerful army. As he had at the lumberyard, Hannibal sensed trouble.

He left the cottage to circle Josephine's property. Along the way, he checked the latches to each of the various gates to make sure they were closed. He tipped the wheelbarrow upside down to keep it from filling with water.

The chickens and other farm animals were resting inside their respective homes or hiding beneath some other shelter. Still, a quiet sense of trouble rumbled through him.

Josephine's house lights were either very dim or completely out. It was late. She could be in bed. However, his sixth sense spurred him on to investigate the strange feeling that something was wrong in Josephine's paradise.

Once in the front yard, he understood his odd sense of disquiet. Cordelia Brennon's dark blue Toyota Corolla was parked beneath the sycamore tree. Lightning cut bold white lines into the cloud-filled sky. The sound of thunder was incredible. It had begun to rain.

He returned to the back of the house, the logical place for him to enter without causing Josephine as much alarm as it would cause her to have him walk unexpectedly through the front door during a heavy storm.

Even though he lived in the cottage, she had extended an open invitation for him to enjoy the kitchen whenever he felt hungry between meals. He chose this way to enter her home. At least she would be prepared for the possibility of his arrival.

Standing in the cool quiet of her kitchen, he registered the lack of recent use in the place where he customarily found her. The fluorescent tube light above the stainless steel kitchen sink was on. There was no bread in the oven or delicious food on the stove. There was no scent of apples or cinnamon.

For the first time in the seven weeks he had known Josephine, this was the only time he had been in her home when she was not there to greet him. The strangeness of the dimly lit kitchen, the darkness of the house, and the blue Toyota Corolla parked in front of Josephine's house made him tense.

He listened hard, his every nerve on end. Thunder broke above the house—*boom*. Lightning struck a tree—*pop*. Power ran rampant through the world—*buzz*. Yet through it all, he heard the distinctive sound of one human being slapping another—*crack!*

A low rumble came from Hannibal, not from his stomach, but from his throat. Something was gravely wrong in this carefully crafted piece of paradise, and the thing that was wrong was Cordelia Brennon. If ever there was a proverbial serpent, she had to be it.

Boom!

Buzz!

Rumble!

Before he breached the living room, a snatch of words stole his breath away.

"I . . . am . . . not . . . Marvella!"

Boom!

"You made me this way."

Buzz!

"I'm your mother."

His heart in his throat, Hannibal watched Josephine fight the demon of her past and the demon of her present: Marvella and Cordelia.

In time, Josephine's gaze left Cordelia's face to meet the eyes of her hero. Again, he had come to her during a time of need. Again, she drew from him the strength to stand up to a woman who, even now, loved her not at all.

Josephine found it hard to get her mind around the word mother or the word aunt. "Go home," she said to the elder Brennon. "Please, just go home."

Hannibal stepped clearly into the living room, fresh red mud leaving the hard print of his boots on the farmhouse floor as he crossed the short distance to Josephine.

Stopping slightly in front of her, his body language rang as clearly as his words. "She's right. It's probably best you head out of here."

Cordelia nearly had a coronary. "How long have you been listening! You . . . you can't just walk in here and tell me . . . you can't . . . get out yourself, you . . . you . . . gigolo!"

Hannibal detached himself from all feeling in order to eyeball the old battle-ax. He had been called many names, but never had he been called a gigolo. The rarity of the moment was priceless. In response, he did the unthinkable. He laughed.

Cordelia came close to spitting fire. Nobody laughed at her and got away with it, nobody at all. She cast frantic eyes about the dimly lit living room. "Where's my pocketbook!"

She raced to the armchair. Pocketbook in hand, she stalked to within inches of Hannibal's mud-stained boots. She whacked his shoulder. "I'll show you a thing or two!" She was Josephine's mother, damn it. No matter what she did, what she said, Cordelia figured she deserved respect. She whacked Hannibal again, determined to make him at least grunt with discomfort.

He did not.

This only made her more angry.

Josephine recognized pure rage when she saw it. The wind howled right along with Cor-

delia's temper. Rain, heavy as the emotions inside the living room, threatened to sweep the
farmhouse straight off its foundation.

Josephine could do nothing about the storm
raging outside. She could do something about
the storm raging inside her house. "Cordelia,
Hannibal will drive you home."

Cordelia's animosity was as corrosive as acid.
"Like hell he's gonna drive me home. I'm not
leaving."

Hannibal's temper over Cordelia Brennon's
you-owe-me attitude was slowly rising. He believed family owed each other nothing but
kindness. He cooled his temper with logic, a
careful, step-by-step process of reason. Reason
dealt with facts, details unaffected by emotion
or circumstance. Facts were truth.

The facts were that Josephine's personal
problems were none of his business. The truth
was that her personal problems were about to
eat her alive. He decided to get rid of problem
number one. He opened the front door. "You
live two minutes from here. It should be no
problem for you to take yourself home."

Cordelia had a hard time containing all the
hatred she had in her body. She pointed at
the scar on Josephine's face. "You deserve everything you get. You're a slut, just like Marvella."

Hannibal's dark eyes flickered over the softly
spoken verbal attack, but he held his tongue.
He believed in facts before instinct, truth be-

fore justice, a belief which centered his identity. For him, integrity was everything.

In his opinion, Cordelia Brennon tampered with facts to make her own brand of truth. From what he had seen and heard, she had no integrity at all. He felt no remorse as he carefully, firmly closed the door in her face.

After she kicked the door, Cordelia stomped down the front steps. From the window, Hannibal watched her run to the Toyota. If the pavement had not been so wet, she would have burned rubber against the asphalt.

He broke the silence with a softly spoken question. "Are you okay?"

"Yeah."

But Josephine was lying. Appalled, she considered what had just happened. She had slapped Cordelia. She was not sure which appalled her the most, the slap itself or the lack of remorse for committing an act considered wrong in any social circle. It shamed her to think Hannibal, the man she had come to view as her hero, had heard part, if not all, of the worst fight she had ever had with Cordelia.

The storm outside continued to reflect the storm inside Josephine. She had no desire to go on living in anger. The truth about Marvella's treachery, the slap against Cordelia's face, and the stark loneliness of her reclusive existence were too much.

It was past time for some drastic changes in her life. Despite her disfigured face, she had to find a way to live whole and free. Drastic change took risk. Suddenly, Josephine was afraid.

Boom!

Crack!

Boom!

She ran up the stairs to her bedroom, her scarred face full of uncertainty. She felt uncertain about the future. If Cordelia was her mother, then her entire life had been a lie.

Boom!

Hannibal kept stride when she flew from the room. His movements decisive, he locked the front door. The living room lights had not been out as he had first suspected; they had merely been on dim. He turned the lights off completely.

In the kitchen, he locked the back door. As he placed his Stetson on the kitchen peg, it occurred to him that when he first arrived in Destiny, he had no more thought on his mind than his own creature comforts—to bunk down for the winter and to rebuild his wallet with cash.

Based upon all he had seen and heard within the walls of Josephine's house, he doubted she would want him around anymore. He knew too much dirt about her. Private woman that she was, it had to tear her stomach up to know he witnessed so dark a period in her life.

Hannibal climbed the stairs to the top floor,

the sound of his boots heavy because he had nothing to hide. Instinctively, he chose the one bedroom out of three that belonged to Josephine.

It was the room with the cracked window, the place she had watched him from as he waited for her to open the front door the first day they met. She was alone then, but not anymore, especially not tonight.

"Josephine?"

No answer.

"Josephine!"

Still no answer.

He opened the door, surprised to see her huddled on the floor in the west corner of her bedroom. Any sort of passion he felt for her body was now buried beneath the weight of his desire to protect her from a fear so great, it had turned a strong, healthy woman into a shuddering child.

"Josephine?"

The word came across softly, sensuously, soothing. The man who spoke it was at a loss about what to do. Again, Hannibal allowed instinct to guide him. Was she afraid of storms? Or was she afraid of an enemy with two legs and a black patent leather pocketbook scratched from years of hard use?

As he contemplated the silent woman, Hannibal remembered the way she had sparked fire at the reverend and his Christian sisters. She had not been afraid of Cordelia Brennon during any time he had witnessed. Tonight, she had been angry, mad enough to strike Cordelia down.

Yet, here she was cowering in her bedroom in a state of panic. The panic was so great that the force of its power pressed her in a corner behind a rocking chair that had seen better days. Hannibal turned off his mind and let his feelings take over.

Off came the work gloves.

Off came the winter jacket.

Off came the western boots.

But seduction was the last thing on his mind. His mind tangled with the certain knowledge that the moment had come to fulfill his first fantasy about the woman who had hired him without asking his name, a woman who trusted him after only a careful study of his calloused hands.

He now used his hands to reach out to her. Gently, protectively, he gathered her against the hard wall of his chest. He knew his heart thundered, but he did not care. She was in his arms, safe, which really was all that mattered.

With Josephine in his arms, Hannibal found himself doing something he had not done since leaving Half Dead: counting time in seconds instead of the seasons. He wanted to cherish that time for as long as she allowed him to touch her.

In turn, she allowed herself to think about what she liked best about him. His total calm soothed her; she fought for serenity, but he lived it.

His question shattered her newfound peace. "Who did this to you, Josephine?"

She said nothing. She knew what he was talking about, only she had no idea where to begin when it came to telling him about her decision to become a recluse.

He took away from her the luxury of silence. "I want to know why you live such a carefully played life. Even though I have no real right, I want to hear all about your scar." He stroked her shoulder. "Tell me."

Maybe the time to tell the whole truth had finally come. Could she trust him? Could she bare her secret, expose her soul? "You'll run when I tell you."

His voice lowered an octave to a level heavy with compassion. "I never run from a fight. I know when to stand my ground, Josephine. This is one of those times." He cupped his hand around the base of her skull, his fingers massaging her, encouraging her. "Who did this terrible thing to you?"

A small shudder marked the beginning of her surrender. More than anything, she needed a friend. "I don't know where to begin."

He rocked her gently. "Anywhere." The tone of his voice assured her that everything would be okay. "Take your time."

Josephine ran her past through her mind.

She had lost her mother not once but twice when Cordelia revealed Marvella was her aunt, not her birth mother.

Marvella this.

Marvella that.

You are just like Marvella.

Josephine had been rejected by Cordelia because the older woman carried a grudge against Marvella's ghost. Cordelia could not accept her sister as a friend, preferring instead to fight her as a rival.

Everybody in Destiny knew about Cordelia's obsession with her sister's life and death. Cordelia was proud, demanding, off-balance, every bit as eccentric as Josephine.

The remaining Brennon women were two circles revolving around the memory of Marvella, but because their circles overlapped with no center, one circle eclipsed the other. Josephine and Cordelia were circles with no center of love.

More than anything, Josephine wanted to be loved. To be worthy of love, she needed to begin anew. All new things were fresh, untried. Maybe it really was destiny which brought Hannibal to her, a man with no past, perhaps the only kind of man with the power to heal her broken heart.

Josephine came out of her reverie with a firmness that let Hannibal know the truth was finally on its way. "Me," she said on a sigh. "I did this to myself."

He stopped breathing.

"Hannibal?"

He opened his mouth, then closed it.

"See?" she mocked. "I didn't think you could handle the truth." She pushed away from his embrace, but he refused to release her, refused to lose any ground between them. Together they stood from the floor.

"You didn't do this by yourself," he argued. "You were a victim, Josephine. That scar on your face is old, which means you were hurt when you were a kid."

She turned in his arms so that her back was to his chest. In front of them was a huge oval mirror trimmed in oak. She met his gaze squarely. There was fear in her eyes. "The ugly in me goes way deeper than the scar on my face."

"I'm not running, Josephine. Tell me the rest."

She wanted to believe him, this man who refused to let her suffer alone. "But you will run."

He led her to the cast iron bed, its quilted cover created years before either of them were born. "No."

Side by side, they sat together, his hands holding both of hers. How easy it would be to lay naked beneath him, to lose herself in his strength, his personal fire.

She wanted to do just that, to be kissed senseless, to forget all about the storm winding down around her. Only now, she felt too vulnerable.

Instead of opening her body to him the way she wanted to do, she opened her mind to him, her memories. She stopped seeing him clearly. Instead, she absorbed the power he offered her. She welcomed it, drew courage from his unflagging generosity. In gratitude, she rewarded him with honesty.

"Before I lived with Cordelia, I lived with Marvella. I remember she cried a whole lot and that we lived poor in a dinky Texas town. My daddy was Stud Bishop. I don't remember him much, except that he was tall and he laughed a lot."

Hannibal's heart stuttered over the name Stud Bishop. He had been fighting the Bishop brothers for no real reason his entire life, especially Mac Bishop, who was every bit as irresponsible as his daddy, Josephine's father. Was the world really that small? "Go on."

"Mama used to tell me stories about this farmhouse. She loved every stick of this place. In fact, this room was her room, right down to the crack in the window."

He squeezed her hands. "Why won't you let me replace that window? Whenever I've brought it up, you've refused. Is it because it reminds you of your mother in some way?"

"She was raped in this room."

Hannibal feared this had happened to Josephine, that she had been sexually molested or physically abused. He imagined that a child could easily grow introverted when left alone to deal with untreated emotional pain. "Raped by who?"

"My dad."

"I can't believe—"

"Which is one reason I kept this ugly business to myself." She leapt to her feet. "Who would believe that a woman would run off with a man who went around raping young girls?"

He pulled her back down beside him, his right thigh touching her left one. "I was about to say"—he paused for emphasis—"that I can't believe the people in this town and I especially can't believe Cordelia."

He had Josephine's attention.

"If Marvella was raped, there may have been others."

"Well, the story gets worse."

Hannibal wondered how that was possible. "Go ahead."

"The night Marvella was raped, Cordelia and the reverend were downstairs talking or whatever."

"You mean, the reverend knows about this?"

"Yeah. See, Cordelia's been crazy about the reverend since dirt was red around here but he's never openly wanted her, and to this day I don't know why. Anyway, the night Marvella said she was raped, Cordelia assumed it was a cover-up for having sex with a grown man for

one thing and with Cordelia's man for another."

"Because Cordelia couldn't have the reverend, she figured she would leave town with
Stud Bishop, the piano player."

"Right."

"Only Marvella really was raped."

"Right."

"At some point during the arguing and
name-calling between the sisters, Cordelia
picked up a brass candlestick and threw it at
Marvella. The candlestick hit the window and
when it did, a piece of the window flew off
and cut Marvella's face. The window was so
thick it didn't break, it just cracked."

"That explains the window."

"There's more."

"The glass from the broken window left a
mark that looked a lot like an X on Marvella's
face. Cordelia said it served Marvella right to
be scarred. She said everybody would ask what
happened to her face and when they did, my
mother—I mean Marvella—would be shamed
into remembering her sin."

"So Marvella ran off with the piano player."

"Not exactly. I think Marvella felt reckless
after the rape. Who would believe her anyway,
especially with her own sister backing the rap-
ist?"

"So Stud Bishop, the piano player, was supposed to be Cordelia's ticket out of Destiny.
Cordelia was probably pregnant with you be-

fore her sister was raped. It's probably what she was really mad about, Josephine. She just took it out on Marvella when she should have been taking it out on Stud Bishop. It's the only scenario that makes any sense."

"That's what I think too." Josephine could not begin to express her gratitude at being able to discuss theories about Marvella's life and death and her own loss of innocence.

For Hannibal, the pieces to Josephine's puzzle clicked into place. "So Marvella stole you from Cordelia out of spite."

"Yeah."

He shook his head. "There's no way to know exactly what happened in the past."

"True, but I'm close."

He sat with his back against the headboard on the full-sized bed, his arms clasped behind his head. "Is that why you're so calm about Marvella not being your mother?"

"At this point, yeah." Josephine's laugh was cynical. "I've spent years trying to figure out why Cordelia hates me so much."

Hannibal drew Josephine beside him, her head against his chest while he stroked the hair at her temple. "It isn't you she hates. It's herself she hates."

Josephine doubted little when it came to Cordelia. "Maybe."

Hannibal listened for the storm. It was gone. "Is that why the Didwiddees took time with you? They guessed the truth?"

Josephine laughed again, still cynical, but more angry this time. "Guess my foot. Everybody in Destiny had to know Cordelia was the one who got pregnant and not Marvella. Cordelia didn't really want me anyway. Maybe that's why Marvella stole me in the first place. Maybe she just wanted somebody to love."

He kissed her forehead. "It's a terrible story."

"It's why I quit going to school."

He remembered friends he had known in Half Dead, kids who dropped out of school because nobody at home cared enough to make them go. "I thought you quit going to school because of your face."

"My face *is* the sordid story. When I was sitting behind the chicken coop with Ivy's little brother all that long time ago, I was sitting back there getting an earful. He told me all kinds of crap about who did what to who. Cordelia caught us and, well, to this day I don't know if she really thought me and Ivy's brother were playing at sex or if she heard him telling me about some of the town gossip going around about the Brennon women. Supposedly we're cursed, you know."

A curse was ridiculous. Hannibal laughed and was pleased she joined him. He ticked off the particulars of the supposed curse. "Let's see. We've got a hell of a case of sibling rivalry. We've got two sad saps for men, the reverend and your father."

"Don't forget my face."

"No one can look at you and not suffer too, Josephine. That the people in this town could refuse to help you either before or after that scar is disgusting to me. The flip side to the Brennon curse is the way the townspeople deal with the curse."

"They ignore it."

"Not entirely. Guilt is a tricky thing."

She fingered the buttons of his red-checkered flannel shirt. "What do you mean?"

"I mean, you've got several guilt-driven neighbors: the Didwiddees, who taught you business; the friends you barter with, who keep down the cost of running your business; and the churches, who buy the food that supplies you with business. We're talking serious team effort here."

He stroked her hair. "When I came to this town, Josephine, I was struck by its eccentric ways. It's not every day a man gets to see horses, cars, tractors, and buggies all on the same street in the middle of the day. With that in mind, I'd have to say anything is possible."

"I don't follow."

"Eccentric towns are made up of eccentric people. I was in a town once where five kids were left orphans. Instead of splitting those five kids up, the town raised them."

"Little kids?"

"No. They ranged from middle to high school age and they didn't want to be split up.

The oldest kid was going to drop out of school to take care of his family. That's when the town stepped in. From food to clothes to college, those kids were looked after by that town of about seven hundred people. Is that what happened to Marvella and Cordelia? Did something happen to their parents and somehow the town stepped in and failed?"

"Something like that. This house belonged to my grandparents. To make a long story short, my grandmother died young, like Marvella. My grandfather couldn't stomach life as a single parent and drifted off. I've never met him."

The puzzle was nearly intact. "Your grandfather was a drifter?"

"I guess. I think that's what Ivy's brother was getting at that day behind the chicken coop. There was a saying around town that Brennon women couldn't hold their men worth the time it took to drink a glass of water."

"That's cold."

Josephine shrugged. "It's true enough. My grandfather drifted off. My father drifted off. The reverend is here, but he may as well be gone for all the stability he provides. He can't commit to anything but meeting Cordelia behind closed doors. The man's a joke."

"Enter one Hannibal Ray, drifter. No wonder Cordelia hated my guts on sight."

Josephine laughed. "She didn't give you a chance at all." The laugh was nervous and shaky, a signal to Hannibal that her spirit had not been destroyed by a lifetime of abuse. He had to know one more thing. "You've told me who marked your face. Now tell me why."

"Spite."

He squeezed her hard, more as a way to scold than to comfort her. They had come too far for half-truths. "It's deeper than that, Josephine. You used a cattle brand."

"How did you know?"

"I'm a ranch hand for hire. I want to know how you got your young hands on an iron cattle brand hot enough to melt your skin."

His anger thrilled her. In the past, people had been angry at her, never for her. "It was easy. At one time, back when my grandfather was around, the Brennon family raised cattle and sheep. Me and Ivy's brother had a game where we heated up the old iron and burned X's on logs from the firewood pile."

He kissed her cheek. This truth was so simple it was not only stunning, but painful.

Josephine scarcely felt his lips against her face. She was deep in the past. "After Cordelia ran off Ivy's brother, she ranted and raved so much about me being like Marvella, I guess I went nuts for a little while. I started screaming and screaming for Cordelia to be quiet, but she wouldn't. She said I was filthy just like Marvella. She said I was a slut. So I . . . I ran over to the hot iron and I jammed it on my face. The thing wasn't steaming hot, or even red hot, but it was hot enough to do what you see now."

He pulled her on top of him. Stroking her back, her head secure in the hollow of his throat, he held her for several minutes before speaking again. "What did she do?"

"Nothing. She plain froze. For once, I'd found a way to shut Cordelia up." Josephine raised up so that she could meet his eyes. "I didn't cry either, Hannibal."

"Is that the spite you were talking about? Even though it hurt, you didn't give Cordelia the satisfaction of seeing you cry?"

"Yeah." Josephine sat up. "Every time she sees me, she sees this scar and she knows she pushed me into doing it."

"You were twelve."

"Huh," she scoffed. "I was an old twelve. You don't grow up the way I did and come out innocent."

"No. You come out strong."

And so it was that in a room made bright with a handmade rug, Hannibal held Josephine in the safety of his arms. Along the way, he fulfilled his favorite fantasy: to hold her tight all through the night.

Josephine woke before dawn. Stiff from being in the same position for a couple of hours, she hurt in every part of her body. "I can't believe we fell asleep."

Hannibal tried to stretch. He groaned his dismay over the cramp in his neck. "Me either."

Turning stiffly, she stared directly at the bridge of his nose. "Thank you."

"Anytime, pretty lady."

Pretty lady.

She scrambled to her feet. Despite her crumpled clothes and tangled hair, she was all fire, all woman. She had told him the truth about herself and he had the nerve to say she was pretty. "Don't you dare patronize me."

Man, she was touchy. "Josephine."

"I will never be pretty."

He thought of her integrity. It took strength to face damning facts. It took courage to build a productive life from the absolute pits of despair the way Josephine had done from the age of twelve. Beauty was not skin deep in her, it was down to the bone. "You are the most beautiful woman I have ever known."

"Get outta my room, Hannibal Ray."

For a hired hand, he was determined to have his say. "I won't leave with you thinking I feel sorry for you. It was a dumb thing you did branding your own face, but it's a kid thing, something done at the spur of the moment without a thought to the consequences."

He refused to budge, no matter what she said, no matter what she did. "Why should you care what I think? You're just gonna leave anyway."

He thought of the many awful things some children witnessed—murder, suicide, beatings, violent accidents. Josephine spent her childhood paying for the cruelty and sins of the people she was born ready to trust. Every adult in her life had failed her, including the Didwiddees. He would not fail her, not now, not ever. "I care."

"Then don't. No matter what lies Cordelia spreads around town, I am not a slut. I don't sleep around. With this stupid scar on my face I'm doomed to live alone for the rest of my life!"

At last, the reason for her reclusive life. The reason was so classic, Hannibal could not believe the idea never once crossed his mind. Josephine lived as a recluse in order to snub the men in town before they could snub her. She snubbed potential friends for the same reason. Her entire adult life was based on showing people she needed no one.

He understood now why he was so keenly in tune with her, why it drove him crazy to think she could take him or leave him: destiny. He could have told her about his mostly average childhood, that he knew exactly where her father lived, but none of it mattered.

None of it mattered because she was at peace with who she was and who she had become. It was this same sense of self, a cold, hard inner light, that allowed her to easily accept the fact that Marvella had never been her true mother.

Josephine needed no man to validate her as a woman. She needed a man to take her for the woman she had become. She was the most self-contained, focused, breathtaking woman he had ever known. No wonder he loved her. "You humble me, Josephine."

The next thing she did shocked them both. She picked up an old-fashioned, solid cast iron and threw it at the crack in the window. The window shattered into a hundred pieces of nothing, as the storm had shattered into nothing.

Hannibal sprang to his feet. "What the . . . ?"

Before he could reach her, she had run down the stairs, through the living room, across the wide foyer, her ponytail flying in the breeze made by her supple young body.

At the instant Hannibal reached the open front door, she flung her feet down the porch steps, across the stone walk to the short gate in a yard where the yellow climbing roses no longer bloomed.

With bated breath, he watched her struggle with the past whose mark she bore against her cheek. Solemnly, he watched her fight this silent battle to rid herself of the red dust and dirt of Destiny.

With his heart in his throat, he watched her lose that silent battle one more agonizing time. The pain he felt for her pierced him to his toes. Hannibal went to the place where the broken woman kneeled on the hard red ground, the exposed flesh of her face wet with the salt of her own tears.

With his heart so far in his throat he could scarcely breathe, Hannibal watched as Josephine closed the latch on the gate of her white picket fence.

SEVENTEEN

The Brennon Farmhouse
Late March

Josephine woke to the sound of splitting wood. It could only be Hannibal. Dressing quickly, she sped down the stairs through the kitchen to see him work.

He was magnificent in his intensity, his system for splitting the wood one of seemingly effortless rhythm. *Whack . . . Whack . . . Whack.* He had been at it for so long, he had built up a dripping sweat. He worked only in a ribbed cotton undershirt, faded jeans, boots, and leather work gloves. He was young, lean, strong, and fit. He appeared tireless.

His muscular legs were set wide for balance. The ax from the weathered gray shed was lifted high in the air, then brought down again with enough force to split the long limb from a fallen oak tree into rounds, the rounds into halves, the halves into quarters. Soon, she would have enough wood to last until the first days of spring.

Spring.

In the spring, he would be gone.

Josephine wanted to run to him, to feel his arms around her once again, yet she stayed where she was, confused and so terribly lonely. It had been weeks since she had confided in him. During all that time, he had been so polite she had wanted to scream.

The only visitors at the farmhouse since the storm were those people directly connected with her food business; Hannibal took care of the rest. Instead of bartering for food or services as a convenience, she now only bartered as a courtesy to those people she had been trading with for years.

Cordelia had not been back, nor had the reverend or his Christian sisters. Hannibal's constant presence, combined with the truth about the Brennon legacy of betrayal, had diminished the power of Josephine's enemies. The tables had turned so that now it was she whom they feared.

Aware Josephine was not taking guff from anyone anymore, concern for their own reputation forced Cordelia and her enemies to ease off their overbearing ways.

It had taken four of them to match the strength of one woman. In contrast, it took the unconditional love of Hannibal to help Josephine discover her true self. She considered the example of excellence he presented to her in his daily walk of life.

He lived without personal or financial debt. His integrity opened doors for him, not simply his wits or his carefree manner. Josephine admired this freedom, and felt again the weight of her reclusive, oppressive life in Destiny.

Soon the daffodils would push through the hard-packed earth to announce the arrival of spring, the beginning of a fresh season of solitude.

Her mind rebelled at living alone again.

In turn, Hannibal continued to split wood like a machine, his thoughts centered on Josephine. The more time he spent with her, the less he felt like leaving her.

Never had she told him she loved him, but it was there in her eyes whenever they lit upon his face, there in the food she painstakingly prepared just for him.

She had him feeling things he had never felt for a woman—the constant desire to keep her safe, the need to know there would always be wood for her home fire, meat for her dining table, and caring arms to hold her when there were storms in the night.

Josephine Brennon was the kind of woman who would welcome him home with hot, tasty food and plenty of it, the kind of woman who would keep a clean house, its door as open to friends as it would be to strangers.

She was the kind of woman who would listen

to his wildest dreams, then help him make those dreams come true. She had what it took to be a fine mother—a big heart, a strong hand, a sound mind, and a loving spirit.

Surely it was love she poured into those silver pots and pans of hers, not just chicken she bartered fresh from neighbors or vegetables she raised from seed in her three-season garden.

She never served food that was less than her best or offered guests anything other than fine linen on good chinaware. Cordelia, Shirley Louise, Bea, and the reverend had enjoyed many a meal fit for the most cherished of friends instead of the longstanding enemies they were. To a drifter, she had given more than room and board. She had given him a home.

During round after round of splitting wood, Hannibal contemplated the present. All the repairs to Josephine's home had been done. There was no reason to wait until the official first day of spring.

He stopped swinging the axe to wipe the sweat from his brow with the back of one forearm. He could leave right now if he wanted to go. He could climb into his old Chevy pickup and drive wherever he pleased, but . . . not just yet, not when he knew he would be leaving his heart behind.

Hannibal split fallen oak wood until his shoulders trembled with fatigue, until Josephine came to him, steaming black coffee and fresh gingerbread in hand, her dark eyes filled with female admiration, the kind of respect that made him feel ten feet tall.

He loved the way she accepted him at face value. She cared nothing about where he came from. If she cared to know where he was going, she felt no need to pry.

He knew now that her don't-give-a-damn shrug really was her way of saying "live and let live." His many years of rambling had been built on this philosophy. It was an irony that as a recluse, she shared the same belief.

She asked for nothing beyond honest labor for an honest wage, and yet . . . Hannibal found himself wishing she would ask him for more. Instead, she stood there staring at him as if he were the only man on the continent and she had no right to ask him to stay.

There was no single person to keep her in Destiny. Cordelia had physically abandoned her. There were no more villains to fight. The Brennon property and farmhouse had been repaired. The boarded second floor window was the only flaw in an otherwise perfect world.

What he said next was unplanned and straight from the heart. "I will always love you, Josephine. Always." It was the second time he had declared his feelings for her, and the second time she kept her feelings about him to herself.

He understood now the pain of Rosalie

Jones's unrequited love, which was now a small yet poetic justice. Unlike Rosalie, Hannibal was prepared to fight for what he wanted. Gently, he chided, "You can't hide here forever, you know."

This she knew. Only she was afraid to leave the safe world she had created for herself. Instead of putting her feelings into words, she used her eyes to tell him how much she cared.

Josephine stared at Hannibal and fell deep into the smooth dark velvet of his voice, into the sweet honesty of his eyes, the healing heat of his soul. She was coming to the . . . end of something. What? She wished she knew.

Josephine was sure of only one thing. "Don't go."

Blood roared through Hannibal's ears. He studied her intently. Her soft body was lush, its language filled with sensuality and power. He was drawn on a primal level to the chemistry that made her uniquely female.

The instinct to chase moved him closer to her body without conscious thought. After all, she had abandoned her pride to beg him to stay. "The future is huge, Josephine. Let's explore it together."

Witnessing Hannibal's display of emotions, the calm purpose in his seen-everything eyes, Josephine was spellbound. There was no other man who came close to arresting her thoughts the way this man did.

Tall, dark, his face fully open for her to

read, he was every good thing she had ever desired. She admired the way he went after exactly what he wanted. It thrilled her to know that what he wanted was her. Need turned her voice husky. "We can stay here."

He took the coffee and still-warm bread from her hands. Sitting the items on a piece of split wood, he was surprised she had not dropped them during their brief, intense conversation.

"You want to stay on this land because staying here means you can go on with your predictable life." He closed the space between them, felt the heat from her body. "You're more than bored, Josephine. It's not just loneliness that you feel."

An odd, very bitter expression covered her face. Her hand leapt to her throat, her gaze sweeping the farmhouse she had loved in place of a human being.

She gazed at the yellow and white house now as if looking for enemies in the shadows. Maybe there were enemies in the shadows, because even now, it was hard for her to let her guard down that one last bit.

"Don't try to analyze me. You don't know me."

"I know all I need to know about you."

She backed away. "Don't humor me."

He stayed in her face. "I don't see the mark on your skin anymore, Josephine. I only see you."

But there was something else she was trying to hide, something obvious. "You want like hell to let your hair down," he whispered gruffly, "only you're scared of that too."

"Don't be silly."

"Prove it." He took her by the shoulders and turned her around. Using his thumb and index finger, he snapped the red rubber band that bound her beautiful hair. He filled his hands with the heavy weight of her hair, brought his nose to it, sniffed it in one heavenly breath. "Damn, you smell good."

"Stop."

"Come here, Josephine."

"No."

"Yes." He framed her face inside the rough palms of his hands. Leaning down, he took everything he wanted in a kiss that said her name was written all over his heart.

It was a good long time before she breathed easily again. He fought her with three weapons she had no answer to: love, pleasure, desire. "You've got no shame."

"None." He kissed her forehead. "I want to come home, Josephine." He kissed her finger on the hand reserved for wedding rings. "Let me in."

Her bones turned to dust. He offered the stability of a committed relationship in an uncertain world. He offered her . . . hope. "Please." Her voice broke, just a little.

"Please what?" he softly countered. "Kiss

you more? Harder? Deeper? Longer? Or should I make love to you the way I want to make love to you?"

Desire ripped through her. "And how is that?"

"All day, every day. I want to see you shine, Josephine."

He trailed a long finger over the X against her left cheek, then slowly, with great reverence, he kissed the exact center of it. He was so tender for a man of his size, so absolutely extraordinary, that the only thing left for her to do was let go.

She laid her forehead against the center of his chest to do something she had not done in fifteen years. She gave herself permission to grieve for a past that had finally been put to rest.

Hannibal lifted her into the brace of his arms, nurtured her with the strength of his body. He carried her into the house, up the stairs and into the room he had not been in since the storm.

He sat with her on the bed, his hands buried in her hair as she poured the tears of her pain into the fabric that covered his chest. The tears branded him in private as surely as the X branded her face.

He looked around her room. It was lean, disciplined, not at all as friendly as the kitchen or even the living room. Josephine's bedroom was functional and practical—as functional and practical as the color brown.

He wanted nothing more than to tear the room down around them. If it was true that the Brennon women were cursed, then it was also true that the curse had its beginning and ending within those four bare and haunted walls.

And still Josephine cried. She cried in deep, ragged sounds of sorrow. She cried as if the world had come to a complete and bitter end. In a way it had.

He finally met a woman with a life all her own no matter how quiet or alone. Josephine thought so little of herself she seldom bothered to primp with pretty women's things. She had tried no wiles on him. Always, she had been her natural self.

For once, Hannibal felt the shame of having nothing substantial to offer a woman. He had no home, no money. Instead, he had something intangible, a code of honor that made him the kind of man who loved only one woman for life.

Josephine deserved better material things than he could give her. However, no man, not one, could love her the way he did. If only she would let him. Already, she was pulling away to dry her tears, to search with intense concentration for a red rubber band.

Hannibal had fought many times before, but

never had he fought for his life. "Don't shut me out, Josephine."

The way he said her name told her there could never be another woman who touched him the way she did. A shot of lust swept through her, shook her out of the rut she had been living in for fifteen years.

With Hannibal, she no longer needed to hide her face in shame. He was right, she did deserve to be loved, but could she walk away from the careful life she had constructed to follow a man she had known for only one season?

Moving in slow motion, as if crossing the twilight haze between earth and sky, he swept her into the brace of his arms to kiss her one last time. He kissed her as if tomorrow might never come, as if two hungry souls had come together at long last. He kissed her as he had kissed few women in his life, with fierce and total abandon.

Hannibal's wet touch did wonderful things to Josephine's tender lips, slick teeth, and hot tongue. Honest with herself, she reveled in every second of his command.

His shoulders overflowed the palms of her hands, the rough thickness of his hair scratching the sensitive skin of her wandering fingers. Enthralled by his masterful hold on her body and mind, she traded kiss for kiss, her toes flexing against the smooth soles of her cowgirl boots.

Josephine's thighs shivered as her stomach flipped in telling, sensuous somersaults. She clung to his shoulder bones, melted against his hard body, forgot who she was and why she stood where she did, wrapped tightly in a stranger's arms; and still, he kissed her forever. Nothing but time lay before or after them. His breath mingled with hers to perfection.

To her mind, Hannibal tasted not only of things forbidden, but of love and honesty and goodness, the three reasons she came back to herself in a crash of emotion. "No!"

"We'd be good together, Josephine." For him, the earth had broken beneath his body, trumpets rang through his ears when he kissed her pretty brown lips. He moved to do it again. Slowly, he slanted his mouth toward hers, inch by delectable inch.

This time she stopped him with a hand against his chest, its muscles teeming with energy, unused and ready to spend on her at her command. If Josephine had said there was someplace else in the world she would rather have been just then, she knew for a fact she would have been telling a lie.

Hannibal would not take no for an answer. Ever so gently, he pulled her into his arms, and there, against every scrap of her better judgment, Josephine gave herself completely, his kiss thrilling her in places seldom ignited.

His seduction was smooth, studied, shattering. Every bit as bold as the hero in classic movies, he eased her willing body over his arm until he was her only support.

One part of Hannibal understood that when a woman said *no* it was time to stop. He knew it was wrong to overwhelm her senses with calculated seduction, especially when he also knew he would feel cheated in some way.

He would feel cheated because he had not waited for her to come to him. For him, patience was not simply the mark of a gentleman, but a way of grace among men. The dilemma of whether to do the right thing—or not—stung his conscience.

He debated in silence. Should he live in the moment? Should he be greedy with his feelings? The internal answer he received was as swift as it was right. The answer was no. He stopped his seduction, broke the kiss, but held his grip.

This time, it was Hannibal who walked away. "I've got to go, Josephine." He had pride too. Josephine had never said she loved him. She refused to compromise and he refused to beg.

Seconds later, she heard the kitchen door open and close. He was leaving Destiny. In minutes, his truck roared to life. Josephine started running.

She reached the gate to her white picket fence just as Hannibal stopped his faded Chevy in front of her. He wore a black Stetson that had seen better days. The unwavering look in his eyes promised a different kind of paradise.

The passenger door, Josephine noticed, had been left open.

He revved his engine.

Josephine took one step. What did she really have to keep her in Destiny? Nothing. She took another step. Another. And then she ran, not bothering to look back. Climbing into her hero's silver truck, Josephine slammed the door closed behind her.

With shaking, determined fingers, she broke the red band holding her long, beautiful hair in check, hair that was identical to the look and style worn by Cordelia until the day she cut it, the same day Josephine burned her own face.

The drifter could not believe his great fortune. He sped away from the white picket fence with its peeling, open gate. His heart was on full, his woman at one with his soul—her hair unbound, flying wild, flying free.

EPILOGUE

Reverend Grady Franklin's church continued feeding the elderly and the homeless. The program was managed by Sister Shirley Louise and Sister Bea.

Cordelia left her two-bedroom bungalow and took residence in the Brennon farmhouse. She replaced the boarded window on the second floor with a stained-glass portrait of the sun. Finally, she placed a stone at the head of her sister's grave. The marble stone read: *Rest in Peace.*

Hannibal and Josephine married in a small Wyoming church. After their first year of marriage, Josephine sent a letter of forgiveness to Cordelia, her only living relative. Cordelia responded with an invitation to return someday to see her again in Destiny.

In time, Hannibal and Josephine took their daughters, Clara and Belle, to visit Cordelia on the Brennon farm. It was Christmas. The white picket fence was gone, but roses bloomed and the grass was still green.

Dear Readers:

It's been a long time since I've had another book released and I hope you feel *Destiny* was worth the wait. A lot has happened between the writing of my two other published books, *Delicious* and *Sensation*. My family moved from California to Oklahoma, where we opened a coffee shop with our cousins, Dee and Brian Stevenson. It's a hectic life we live these days, getting a new business off the ground. The rewards of small business ownership are profound and not always defined by dollar signs. It feels good to start something fine from scratch, which is exactly why we traded the big city for small-town living. I feel proud that we had the nerve to set down new roots. It's what *Destiny* is all about.

I hope you will write me regarding *Destiny* when you have the time. I answer all letters that I receive, and ask that you please be patient when it comes to your response because it will definitely be coming. I can be reached at the address below. I look forward to hearing from you soon.

Shelby Lewis
P.O. Box 253
Guthrie, OK 73034

Sincerely yours,
Shelby Lewis

ABOUT THE AUTHOR

Shelby and her husband, Steve, live in the mid-southwest with their sons, Steven and Randal. A bookworm at heart, she enjoys reading mystery and romance novels. In her free time, she likes to garden and watch classic films.

Coming in May from Arabesque Books . . .

__JUST BEFORE DAWN by Rochelle Alers
1-58314-103-0 $5.99US/$7.99CAN
When district attorney Sara Sterling returns to her childhood home in New Mexico and meets her enigmatic neighbor Salem Lassiter, she is confronted with an inescable passion. But when a series of mysterious "accidents" threaten her life, the two must fight to claim a love that promises always.

__ILLUSIONS OF LOVE by Marcia King-Gamble
1-58314-104-9 $5.99US/$7.99CAN
Journalist Skyla Walker is uneasy about her latest assignment—investigating famous illusionist Creed Bennett and the disappearance of several women in his town. But as Skyla searches for truth, she discovers a sensual attraction to Creed . . . can their love be more than an illusion?

__SECRETS OF THE HEART by Marilyn Tyner
1-58314-105-7 $5.99US/$7.99CAN
To escape her father, Amanda Reynolds accepted Drew Connors' offer of platonic marriage—and then ignored the growing love she felt for him and struck off on her own. Years later, Amanda and Drew meet again . . . and discover a re-ignited passion that burns even brighter than before . . .

__A VERY SPECIAL LOVE
by Janice Sims, Courtni Wright, Kayla Perrin
1-58314-106-5 $5.99US/$7.99CAN
There is nothing like a mother's devotion—or a mother's heart. Spend an unforgettable day with three of Arabesque's best-loved authors and discover the wonderful power of mothers in love.

Call toll free **1-888-345-BOOK** to order by phone or use this coupon to order by mail. *ALL BOOKS AVAILABLE May 1, 2000.*

Name _____

Address _____

City _____ State _____ Zip_____

Please send me the books I have checked above.

I am enclosing	$_____
Plus postage and handling*	$_____
Sales tax (in NY, TN, and DC)	$_____
Total amount enclosed	$_____

*Add $2.50 for the first book and $.50 for each additional book.
Send check or money order (no cash or CODs) to: **Arabesque Books, Dept. C.O., 850 Third Avenue, 16th Floor, New York, NY 10022**
Prices and numbers subject to change without notice.
All orders subject to availability.

Visit our Web site at **www.arabesquebooks.com**